THOSE WHO WATCH
OVER THE EARTH

THOSE WHO WATCH OVER THE EARTH

By Daniel Sernine

Translated by David Homel

Black Moss Press

© 1990 this translation David Homel

During the translation of *Those Who Watch Over the Earth,* the author took the opportunity to make certain changes to his original work.

Published by Black Moss Press
1939 Alsace St., Windsor, Ontario
N8W 1M5.

Black Moss Books are distributed in Canada and the United States by Firefly Books, Ltd., 250 Sparks Avenue, Willowdale, Ontario, M2H 2S4.

Financial assistance toward publication of this book was gratefully received from the Canada Council and the Ontario Arts Council.

COVER DESIGN BY BLAIR KERRIGAN/GLYPHICS
COVER ILLUSTRATION BY AMANDA DUFFY

Typesetting and page design by Kristina Russelo

Printed and bound in Canada.

Canadian Cataloguing in Publication Data

Sernine, Daniel
[Organisation Argus. English]
Those who watch over the earth

(Young readers' library)
Translation of: Organisation Argus.
ISBN 0-88753-214-4

I. Title. II. Title: Organisation Argus. English. III. Series.
PS8587.E7707413 1990   jC843'.54   c90-090409-7
PZ7.S37th 1990

Table of Contents

Chapter One
The Experiments of Doctor Guillon

Marc Alix left the Cardiological Institute feeling lost and overwhelmed. He hadn't expected good news: he'd known for quite a while about his congenital heart defect, and that he'd have to spend the rest of his days avoiding sports and exertion.

But now he'd been told that his life might be cut short. He was fifteen, and the doctor had let him know, as tactfully as possible under the circumstances, that he would be very lucky to reach the age of twenty.

Marc's ailment was extremely rare. Basically, his heart was unable to develop at the same rate as the rest of his body. Being smaller than normal, the organ was forced to pump blood more quickly, and the effort had simply worn it out before its time.

Marc's heart could not deal with the increased flow of blood required for the slightest physical exercise. The defect couldn't be corrected surgically. It would have taken a heart transplant to cure him, but that was out of the question. Between 1967 and the mid-seventies, not a single transplant patient had survived, due to the phenomenon of organ rejection.

Marc was condemned to die. Something that he'd always dimly considered would happen one day, but Marc was going to die at the age of twenty, and that he couldn't consider. He was deeply troubled by this thought, filled with the sinking despair of those who must stand face-to-face with death.

And he was alone. His mother had died when he was nine. His father was a successful businessman in the construction industry. The day of Marc's appointment at the Cardiological Institute, Mr. Alix hadn't found the time to accompany his son to the Institute. It sometimes seemed that Marc wasn't as important to his father as an only son should be.

To tell the truth, Mr. Alix's feelings for Marc were difficult to gauge. He wasn't exactly indifferent to the boy, but he didn't show much warm affection, either. Mr. Alix had always dreamed of healthy, robust sons, athletes who would make him proud. Instead, he'd ended up with a boy who, behind a well-nourished facade, concealed a debilitating weakness.

Marc took after his mother. He was fair-haired, a little too fragile, a little too mild-mannered. But most of all, he was too smart. Every time Mr. Alix felt the weight of Marc's sober gaze, every time he listened to the boy's big words and complicated notions, Mr. Alix couldn't shake the feeling that Marc was making fun of him, scoffing because he wasn't all that bright, because he lacked refinement and taste.

People all too often noted, even in his father's presence, that Marc took after his mother and the Guillons more than the Alix side of the family. Given the choice, Mr. Alix would have preferred not to look after this son, and worry constantly about his health, and pretend to be interested in his studies, and hide his own less refined tastes for fear of the boy's scorn.

Marc paid him back in kind. He had never been overly fond of his gruff, loud father, and as the years passed, he came almost to hate him. As for his stepmother, the woman his father married two years after the death of his first wife, Marc felt a cool neutrality towards her. She was both vain and foolish, always trying to seem busy when in reality her whole existence was empty and vacuous.

The only person Marc loved was his uncle and godfather, Doctor Horace Guillon. He was a short man in his fifties, whose grey hair was already fading to white. Horace Guillon had no children of his own and treated Marc like a son.

Marc, who was only fifteen years old, was already studying masters-level courses at the Montreal Polytechnical School. He had the misfortune to be what is commonly called a "boy genius." Nature had blessed him with exceptional brain power, and fate had given him an ambitious mother. During her life she had pushed him in his studies the way a trainer pushes a thoroughbred horse at the race-track.

Marc was surrounded by students ten or fifteen years his senior. With the heavy course load, he found little time to seek out friends his own age.

* * *

It was the beginning of April when Marc learned he had only four or five years to live. For days he was utterly downcast, and even neglected his course-work. Everything in his life had lost its meaning. Eventually, he began to take up his normal routine again, if only to escape from his gloomy thoughts. Somehow, he resigned himself to his fate, determined not to waste his last years in idleness.

Marc was only a part-time student at the Polytechnical School, with only two courses. Uncle Horace supervised his studies. He had also secured his nephew a position as research assistant at the Freeman Foundation, so the boy could help him with his work. The Freeman Foundation was a privately run organisation specialising in neurological research.

Dr. Guillon was studying electrical currents in the brain and their disturbances, such as epilepsy. Very low-level electrical currents, identified by their frequencies — either delta,

10

theta, alpha, mu or beta — crisscross the healthy human brain. In an epileptic patient, these frequencies are jumbled and irregular, causing the seizures that characterise the disorder.

When Marc started work at the Foundation, Horace Guillon was putting the finishing touches on a system able to influence brain waves and normalise cerebral disturbances. To explain it as simply as possible, Dr. Guillon had developed a type of electromagnetic wave, called kappa, to match certain electrical pulses in the brain.

Even in the initial stages of his research, Dr. Guillon had suspected that his kappa waves could be used for dubious ends. He had cloaked his experiments in the utmost secrecy, working alone for the most part and confiding only in his nephew. Kappa waves could be used to help epilepsy patients, but they could also be abused. Using kappa waves, one could conceivably control people's moods from a distance without their ever realising it, making them listless and passive, or aggressive and overexcited, or even incoherent and hysterical.

Horace Guillon hadn't yet refined his system to such a degree of subtlety. It would take a lot more work to reach that point. Still he could imagine what would happen if the police or the army got their hands on his system and decided to use it on the population — a crowd of demonstrators, for instance, or a group of university students, or even a whole sector of

11

the city. Such a thing wasn't feasible yet, but Dr. Guillon couldn't help thinking about those possibilities.

Dr. Guillon had been very worried during the last few months and had spoken to Marc about his concerns. He wondered if people were spying on him. He turned his laboratory upside down in search of hidden eavesdropping devices, but had found nothing. Still, in the office, he spoke to his young assistant in a low voice.

Horace Guillon wanted to avoid the possibility that his kappa waves would be used as tools of repression or provocation; he was even seriously considering putting an end to his experiments. "Science is never neutral," he told Marc. "In the world today, scientists are all too often manipulated by big corporations or the military. The result of years of their labour can be taken from them, and they can't say a word. Or, if scientists themselves lack judgment, they can succumb to pressure and work voluntarily for dubious ends."

One day at the end of April, Doctor Guillon went to speak to Charles Regnier, the director of the Freeman Foundation. He wanted to explain his quandary over continuing work on the kappa waves project. Regnier was very soothing. He said he understood the doctor's concern, but tried to convince him to continue in the interest both of science and of the Foundation.

"You've got to understand," he told Dr. Guillon, "that our Foundation is utterly dependent on the grants we receive. If our research doesn't produce results, or if it doesn't seem to be going anywhere, our sponsors will stop their support."

"That's precisely what I wanted to ask you about," said Guillon. "I learned that the Foundation is supported by government money. Exactly how much do they give us?"

Regnier seemed embarrassed, but quickly regained his composure. "Their contribution is quite modest, Doctor. Hardly worth mentioning."

Horace Guillon was unconvinced. Regnier had concealed the fact that the government was involved with the Foundation. He could just as easily hide the extent of that involvement. "You understand," he explained, "that I can't continue in good conscience to work for an organisation that depends on the government. I'd be too worried that the statet would step in and take over my research, especially since it can be used for non-medical ends."

"Your fears are exaggerated," Regnier tried to reassure him. "This is a free country. The government would never deliberately misuse a medical invention."

"Perhaps the government wouldn't. But everyone knows they're not entirely accountable for the army or the police, and they often exceed the limits of the law without the government suspecting a thing."

Their discussion stopped there, with Regnier advising his colleague to think carefully about the problem. "Today is Thursday," he said. "Think it over this weekend and come see me Monday. I know you're a reasonable man. I'm sure you'll decide to continue your work for the general good of the Foundation, which has done so much to support you in your research."

But Doctor Guillon was still doubtful when he returned to his office. Marc was waiting for him.

"You seem worried, Uncle."

The doctor usually confided in Marc because he respected him so much. This time he wanted to be certain that his words remained confidential. He switched on a tape recording of a speech he had once given and turned up the volume, just in case there was a microphone hidden somewhere in the office. Then he stood close to Marc and spoke in a low voice.

"Regnier admitted that the government funds the Foundation, but he claims the sum isn't significant. I wasn't convinced. I wouldn't be surprised if the Feds were the primary or even the only source of money here. Imagine what would happen if the Army or the RCMP got their hands on my invention. Regnier sure wouldn't step in to defend me. He's the type who'd gladly offer up my work. The Army may already know about my research. No, I really think I'm going to stop my research."

* * *

Meanwhile, Charles Regnier was in his office discussing the situation over the telephone with Major Ben Gagnon, an officer in the Army's "security services" for the Montreal region.

"Doctor Guillon is giving me trouble," said Regnier.

"Guillon, Guillon.... The one doing the kappa wave stuff?"

"That's him. He just left my office. He's having second thoughts about continuing his research."

"Is he serious?"

"I think so. I've suspected this might happen for some time now. He's discussed it with his nephew before."

"Could the work be continued by his colleagues?"

"That's the problem. He's never let a technician get involved in his research. He's always worked alone."

"Doesn't he send you reports on a regular basis?"

"His reports leave out most of the details. When I question him on his work, he's very vague."

"You're telling me Guillon is indispensable."

"If he left us, we'd have to spend a good two years on research before we reached his

15

level of knowledge in the area."

"What if we increased his salary? Would that convince him to stick with the work?"

"My God, absolutely not! It would probably offend him."

"Then we'll have to exert some pressure. Like every human being, he's got to have a weak spot. Does he have a wife? Kids?"

"He's a widower. Never had children."

"No other family?"

Regnier was reluctant. "He's got a nephew. His godson. He seems very attached to the boy."

"There we go. How old is the kid?"

"Fourteen or fifteen."

"Perfect! An age at which people are likely to do foolish things."

"What are you going to do?"

"Leave it to me. After all, it's my job. If Guillon loves this kid the way you say, he'll probably do anything to get him out of trouble."

"You're not going to blackmail him," Regnier objected.

"Listen, I'm not asking for your permission, Regnier. I know how important your job is to you, so just give me the info I need on the boy, and we'll call it a day."

Regnier gave in without much resistance to the major's demands. He was a practical man, and he knew that if he lost his directorship he'd be hard pressed to find new work. He had a few skeletons in his own closet.

Chapter Two
Conflict Erupts

Marc left Doctor Guillon's office that Thursday and went home for lunch. The latest issue of a UFO magazine he subscribed to was waiting for him in the mail.

Marc had been interested in UFO's — Unidentified Flying Objects — ever since one summer night he'd spent in the Lake Megantic region. That night, he'd seen a light in the sky. He was thirteen at the time, on vacation in the Eastern Townships.

That night he'd stayed outside particularly late to observe Jupiter with a small stargazer's telescope. Something crossed the sky at high speed, coming from the northwest and heading towards the state of Maine, whose border wasn't far away. The flying object was visible too long for it to be a shooting star. It was also too fast to be a man-made satellite, and its trajectory was clearly earthward.

It was a white glimmer, somewhat bluish. It was weak and diffuse, not at all clear in outline like Jupiter, for example. It seemed to come from a great altitude, and fell rapidly to earth in a straight line. It couldn't have been a meteor falling to Earth because, soon after Marc spotted it, it gradually slowed its descent. The pale blue glimmer grew brighter, shining as white as Venus as it neared the earth. It brought to mind a space ship, igniting its retrorockets to slow down. That's what Marc concluded. It was a bona fide UFO. A space ship from another solar system. The sighting lasted only a few seconds. Then the light then disappeared behind a ridge of mountains across the border in Maine.

Marc told no one about the bizarre experience except his uncle. Horace Guillon listened carefully and never questioned whether his nephew was telling the truth. The doctor himself believed in UFO's. He'd never seen one, but he was convinced that extra-terrestrial beings navigated the skies.

Since that summer night, Marc often thought about extra-terrestrials who, it seemed, observed and visited the planet Earth. He wondered about their motives, and decided they were probably benevolent. He started to read books and magazines on the subject.

That Thursday afternoon, the weather was warm and inviting. After his courses ended he found a spot on the terrace in front of the university's main building and sat down to read his magazine. He'd just begun when someone tapped him lightly on the shoulder. It was Carl Andersen, a student in his first year at the Polytechnical School.

"What are you reading, friend?" he inquired.

He always called Marc "friend", and indeed, Carl was perhaps his only friend. He looked eighteen or nineteen years old, and wore fairly long blond hair. He spoke with a heavy accent. Marc deduced he was German or Scandinavian from his name. He couldn't have been in Canada too long, because he wasn't all that familiar with local customs. He didn't always understand things people said, and often had to ask someone to explain.

Marc had known him for several months, but rarely saw him because they were in different years and shared no classes. Marc was so tied up with his studies and his work that he rarely went out and had no friends his own age. There was certainly no chance of meeting another fifteen-year-old at the Polytechnical School. His classmates had a whole range of attitudes towards him. Some of them told him how much they admired his IQ — a reaction which irritated Marc no end. Others were paternalistic, teasing him with jokes that weren't always in the best of taste. A few seemed jealous, especially if they themselves weren't making the grade.

Carl was different. He approached Marc as if it were normal to find a fifteen-year-old in university. He rarely brought up the exceptional nature of the boy's situation. Unlike the others, Andersen never spoke of his courses or studies. He talked about science fiction and the wonders man could accomplish if only he put his knowledge to wise use. He could wax philosophical about matters of ecology or world peace. One of his favourite ideas was that there should be a superior authority overseeing the great powers and intervening to prevent war and irreversible pollution.

Marc loved to talk to Carl because these subjects fascinated him. Most of the time, he found himself agreeing with the young man.

That day he showed Carl the UFO magazine and asked whether he believed in such things.

"Sure I believe in them," Carl answered. "Many of the sightings are mistakes, but a good number are valid."

Marc told about his own experience at Lake Megantic, a story he'd kept to himself until then. Then he concluded, "Those extra-terrestrials who watch over us, I think they should intervene from time to time, to straighten out some messes here on Earth."

"Who says they don't?" Carl replied.

"You think so?"

"Who knows? Maybe they're not even extra-terrestrials."

"You think they're humans?" Marc asked in surprise.

"Imagine a group of scientists and technicians acting unbeknownst to governments around the world. What if they attained a level of technological prowess far beyond that of the superpowers?"

"Advanced enough to manufacture those mysterious flying objects?"

"Why not?" said Carl. "It's not impossible."

Marc nodded slowly. It was a hypothesis he'd entertained without really believing it. Andersen seemed to take it seriously enough.

The two friends discussed the idea at length. That night, Marc dreamed of space ships watching over Earth and hurtling through the solar system. Recently he'd had quite a few dreams like this, but he could never remember the details in the morning.

* * *

By Monday morning, Horace Guillon still hadn't changed his mind about discontinuing his research for the Foundation. In fact, he was more resolved than ever to suspend his study of kappa waves. He planned to announce his decision to Director Regnier first thing that day.

He returned from that meeting red with anger and breathing in short, laboured gasps. His hand was on his chest, as if he was in pain.

Marc, who was sitting in the office as he did almost every morning, immediately asked, "You had an argument with the Director?"

The Doctor didn't answer right away. He poured a glass of water and swallowed two pills. His health wasn't good and over-excitement was dangerous for his heart. Alarmed, Marc noticed that his uncle's hands were trembling.

Guillon motioned for the boy to accompany him into the next room, a small laboratory reserved for his exclusive use. No one was there to listen in on their conversation, but the doctor suspected a microphone was hidden somewhere nearby. One of the electrical instruments Guillon used for his experiments produced static interference on radios and television sets. Every time Doctor Guillon wanted to speak absolutely confidentially, he used this apparatus to distort the reception of any microphone that might have been planted for purposes of spying. As soon as the machine started to hum he exclaimed, "I should have suspected it! The Freeman Foundation is heavily financed by the government — more specifically by the Defence Department. Regnier admitted that the Army and the RCMP were very interested in my work. He even hinted they were very keen for me to continue what I've started. I wouldn't be surprised if the CIA knew about it, too!"

While he spoke, the doctor took a screwdriver and began to detach the back panel of a small computer. The computer was programmed to analyse electrical currents in the brain and adjust kappa waves to match these frequencies.

Marc paled as he realised how right his uncle's fears had been. The confidentiality of his work had been violated.

The doctor tried not to raise his voice, despite his obvious anger. "Regnier as much as ordered me to continue my work. But he has no real authority over me. Not only do I plan to quit the Foundation, but I'll also destroy the main elements of my system."

"They'll sue you for sure."

"Let them try! They'll get their share of unwanted publicity, I can promise you that much. It would embarrass the government if I went public with this scandal."

Horace Guillon took a pair of pliers and began extracting transistors and resistors, cutting wires, smashing switches and contacts. His nephew watched him in dismay, not daring to move.

"They can't continue this work without me," the doctor said. "None of the technicians or researchers who have cooperated with me ever got a thorough understanding of the system. Not one of them has any complete notion of how I operate, and I haven't given much away in my written reports. If I sabotage the equipment, they'll have three long years of work just to get to the point where I am today."

* * *

In the meantime, Regnier hurried to report on events to Major Gagnon.

"Finally! I've been trying to get a hold of you for the last hour. Doctor Guillon wants to resign."

"So he's playing the rebel, is he? We'll have to seize his notes in case he tries to leave with them."

"I searched his office last night and couldn't find anything of value. But he does have a microfiche machine. He's so secretive, he probably had all his important documents transcribed onto microfiche. God knows where he hides them. They'd be small enough to fit in an envelope."

"They're probably at his house," Major Gagnon said. "He's already being followed by one of my men. I'll put another guy on his trail and get two more to search his home. I'll bet he's been contacted by foreign powers."

"Personally, I wouldn't think so."

"Anyway, I'll get the RCMP to search his place right away, while he's still in his office. He's still there, I hope?"

"Yes. I told him to think it over and that I'd pay him a visit in the early afternoon. Maybe you should come. I'm out of arguments to change his mind. I need your expertise."

"Don't worry, Regnier. We're putting together some very convincing arguments."

* * *

Horace Guillon was taking apart the kappa wave modulator whose function was to influence electrical currents in the brain with the aid of a special transmitter. Marc had joined in, with a heavy heart, to help in the destruction. He was dismantling the transmitter with his uncle. It tore him apart to have to ruin the fruit of such long labours. But he supported his uncle and would have acted in exactly the same way in his position.

"When you've finished," the doctor said, "get to work on the encephalograph machine."

The electro-encephalograph is an instrument that measures electrical impulses in the brain. Doctor Guillon's machine was specially adapted for his purposes, and very sophisticated.

The uncle and nephew worked away at these gems of technology with pliers and screwdrivers until they lay in ruins on the laboratory floor. Doctor Guillon's system comprised four principal instruments whose fine-tuning had taken months, if not years, to accomplish. All that remained of his work were the numerous plans and sketches that Guillon kept in his files.

"What will you do with your notes?" Marc asked.

"Ah," Doctor Guillon replied, "my notes. They'd love to get their hot little hands on those, but good luck to them!"

25

His research notes, diagrams, computer programmes and working documents had been reproduced in microfiche form by a private company, without the knowledge of anyone at the Freeman Foundation. Each microfiche was eight centimetres by thirteen, manufactured from ultrafine transparent plastic. Each contained sixty pages of text, tables or illustrations. The sum total of Horace Guillon's kappa wave research was to be found in two ordinary-sized envelopes. He kept one in the inner pocket of his suit jacket, and tucked the other away in a small safe in his house.

He whispered to his nephew, "For several days now I think someone's been tailing me. Perhaps an agent from the Army's security services. If my hunch is right, I'm in far deeper trouble than I suspected. Early this morning I took the envelope with the microfiches from my safe and hid it."

"Are you sure you weren't followed?" Marc asked.

"Positive. I was very careful. And I'll tell you where I hid the envelope. If things turn ugly, the microfiche must be destroyed. Do you remember the location of my wife's grave in the Notre Dame des Neiges Cemetery?"

"More or less."

"Good. The envelope is buried at the foot of the tombstone, on the left hand side, between the stone and the earth, about twenty centimetres down."

The doctor's words frightened Marc. Suddenly he asked, "What do you mean, `if things turn ugly?' Do you think you'll be hurt?"

At first, the doctor didn't reply. Marc had never seen him so agitated. Finally the old man said, "Yesterday I would have laughed if you'd suggested I was in personal danger. Today I'm not so sure. All kinds of people seem to be intrigued by my work: the Army, the RCMP, maybe even the CIA. Each of these outfits is interested in using kappa waves for strategic purposes."

The uncle and the nephew had finally finished their work of destruction. They'd removed every microchip. Guillon collected them and put them in a small metal garbage can with several pages of crumpled newsprint. He threw a lit match in, and the paper curled with flame.

"You have school this afternoon," the doctor said. "It's time for you to leave. I'll let you know what happens."

Just then, someone knocked on the office door and the intercom started to buzz. Guillon turned off the machine that he used to create static interference, then answered the call. It was his secretary.

"The Director and another man are here to speak with you."

"Ask them to wait one moment."

"They say it's urgent."

"They can wait!"

He turned off the intercom and whispered to Marc, "Regnier has brought someone. Probably a government man, maybe someone from the military. They'll trot out all kinds of patriotic nonsense about national security. They're reacting much more quickly than I'd anticipated."

The words were barely out of his mouth when the knocking started up again, this time with insistence. The doctor threw a few more sheets of paper in the waste basket and said, "The doors to my office and to the laboratory are locked. They can knock as long as they want."

The door shook with each blow, and an angry voice called, "Open up, Doctor! What are you up to in there?"

Things were heating up. The doctor fumbled in his jacket pocket and pulled out the envelope containing the first series of micro-fiches. He emptied it into the flaming waste basket and signalled to Marc to leave.

"Will they threaten you?" asked Marc.

His uncle grabbed him by the shoulders and pushed him towards the back door, whispering, "Hurry. And don't forget to dispose of the hidden microfiche if things look bad."

Marc didn't want to leave. He was worried about his uncle's ailing heart. The intruders had made it to the office and were shaking the laboratory door. The Director must have a pass-key allowing access to all the offices.

"Doctor Guillon, open up!"

"Go on, get out of here!" whispered

Guillon, pushing his nephew out the second laboratory door.

"Be careful of your heart," Marc said. "Don't get carried away!"

The boy found himself alone in the service corridor, speaking to a closed door. With a heavy heart he made his way out of the building, fervently that his uncle wouldn't come to harm.

* * *

That very night Marc learned of his uncle's sudden death. Director Regnier phoned the house to break the news. Horace Guillon, he said, had died suddenly of a massive heart attack, and all efforts to revive him had been in vain. The Director was rather vague about the circumstances surrounding the death, but it didn't take much imagination for Marc to reconstruct the scene. A fresh dispute must have arisen between Regnier and the doctor. Perhaps they tried to threaten or blackmail him. His uncle would have been enraged and that would have been enough to bring on heart failure.

Marc took refuge in his bedroom. He was torn between his anger at those who caused his uncle's death, and an engulfing sadness at the loss of a man he'd loved like a father.

He dreamed of avenging the doctor's death. But how could he tackle such powerful adversaries? His uncle was right to predict that things would turn ugly, but Marc had never imagined they'd end so tragically. The most he could do, he decided, was to destroy the second series of microfiches. That way, at least his uncle's murderers wouldn't be rewarded with success.

But all that would come later. For now, Marc was too upset to take concrete action at all.

Chapter Three
Dreams

It was Wednesday evening. Marc was in bed, tossing and turning, unable to sleep. He hadn't slept a wink Monday night, he'd dozed fitfully Tuesday, and that night it seemed sleep wouldn't come any more easily. He kept picturing the anxiously peaked face and nervous gestures of his uncle several hours before his death. He mulled over the intrigue surrounding Doctor Guillon's work on kappa waves.

That morning Marc learned from another uncle that Doctor Guillon's house had been ransacked by unknown intruders Tuesday, the day after his death. It seemed they'd done a thorough search, without bothering to put things back in order before they left. Marc thought that this was the work of the RCMP, searching for the microfiches.

That day, Wednesday, while Marc was at the funeral parlour and his parents were out, Marc's room, in turn, was searched. Everything had been rifled — closet, chest of drawers, books, and in particular the filing cabinet where

Marc kept his class notes. Marc noticed traces of the intrusion that evening; many of his possessions weren't in their usual place. Marc wished he could talk about it to his father, but he didn't say anything, since he had no material proof. Besides, he had no desire to divulge the entire story.

It was clear that the RCMP was hot on the trail of the hidden microfiches. Marc would have to act quickly to dispose of them. Horace Guillon had specifically asked that they be destroyed "if things got ugly." Had he foreseen that they would get ugly to the point of his own death? The least Marc could do was fulfil his final wish.

It was easier said than done, of course. The Alix household was under surveillance. Across the street Marc could see a car parked in almost the exact spot it had been Tuesday night. From time to time, the man at the wheel glanced toward the house. On a second street — the house was on a corner — another man waited patiently in another parked vehicle. Marc hadn't noticed him the night before, but he was pretty sure it was more surveillance.

It was impossible to leave the house without being followed. Marc went to bed, giving up on his project for the night. But he had already thought of ways to shake off his cover and accomplish his mission.

His exhaustion from the previous two days finally caught up with him and gradually he felt his limbs grow heavy. He was in the twilight zone between consciousness and sleep when the visions came to him.

The visions had haunted his nights for some weeks now. Usually they came just as he was about to fall asleep, and sometimes during sleep itself. They didn't come every night. Marc had only a vague recollection of them when he awoke. It was as if desires that he hadn't been aware he possessed were awakening in him. New feelings of certainty were taking hold, bit by bit. For example, he was now convinced that Earthlings were not the only intelligent life in the solar system, and that other human beings watched over those who lived on Earth, just like Carl Andersen had suggested. More and more, Marc was filled with the desire to leave his world and visit other planets. These were ideas that had come to him from time to time, just as they did to most adolescents living in the space age, but they seemed so urgent, so insistent now.

That night the visions were less vague and they lingered in his memory. Images moved before his half-opened, weary eyes in the very space of his dark bedroom.

The planet Earth, a blue globe, was floating in the air just above Marc's bed. Huge space ships orbited, just barely visible, observing the planet. Then Marc saw a rough landscape and he knew somehow that it must be the dark side of the moon. There, on the slope of high mountains, an underground base sheltered vast rooms where hundreds of screens depicted scenes of life on Earth.

Then, still lying safely in bed, Marc had the vivid sensation of speeding through space. He reached the asteroid belt, beyond the orbit of Mars. He discovered a tiny, hollow planet. Beneath its rocky surface, a breathtakingly advanced civilisation flourished in secret. A new culture was thriving amid fairyland gardens sheltered under transparent domes. The boy took it all in willingly, without surprise. He was in that semi-conscious state where reality becomes blurred and hazy.

Once again Marc leaped into the void, towards the very limits of the solar system. Jupiter and her moons passed by overhead, like a balloon and so many glowing marbles floating through his bedroom. As he passed through the orbits of the outer planets, he crossed paths with space ships. Finally, beyond Pluto, he saw great vessels being built to conquer the stars.

The Milky Way stretched across the boy's room, glimmering in icy mystery. At long last, Marc gave into sleep, his head brimming with these vivid and fantastic scenes.

* * *

The funeral was on Thursday morning. During the burial, Marc, who stood in the first row, couldn't take his eyes off the spot where the second set of microfiche was supposed to be hidden at the foot of the tombstone, close to the gaping pit ready to receive Horace Guillon's coffin.

Marc's throat was tight with emotion, but his eyes were dry. He'd cried himself out the night of the death and had no tears left. As he watched the proceedings, he couldn't help thinking that in a few years it would be his turn to disappear into the bowels of the Earth in a nice varnished coffin. These days it was common for a man in his fifties to die of heart failure. But for a youth just reaching his prime, it would be a far greater tragedy.

Among those present at the burial, Marc spotted the director of the Freeman Foundation, Charles Regnier. He was responsible for Horace Guillon's death, and he had the nerve to show up at the funeral and pretend to grieve. The day before at the funeral parlour, Marc had noticed Regnier conversing at length with his father and stepmother. That evening, Mr. Alix had asked Marc whether he intended to remain at the Freeman Foundation where, according to him, a "brilliant career" lay before him. Marc guessed that Regnier had planted this idea in his father's mind.

After the ceremony was over and the casket had been lowered into the waiting grave, the mourners filed past the relatives, shaking hands and whispering condolences on their way out of the cemetery. Marc stayed by the grave site for a long while, trying to decide whether to risk retrieving the hidden micro-fiche. He realised that even if he waited till the last mourner left, it was risky to attempt it in broad daylight.

Marc wandered over to the line of cars waiting on the road several meters off. Just as he was squeezing by one of the vehicles, he felt a hand fall heavily on his shoulder. It was Charles Regnier, uttering condolences and then, unexpectedly, inviting Marc to join him in his car for a private chat. Marc had no desire to speak to him, but Regnier opened the door and pushed him in gently, insisting. Marc climbed in against his will, and Regnier sat beside him on the front seat.

Marc noticed a second man sitting quietly behind them. Perhaps he was one of the Director's colleagues. The man uttered a terse greeting.

Regnier closed the door and spoke, trying to be affable, "You know everyone at the Foundation deeply regrets your uncle's passing away."

"Sure," thought Marc bitterly, gritting his teeth. "The only thing you regret is not getting your hot little hands on his invention."

"We'd like to preserve your uncle's memory," the Director continued, "by developing some of the ideas he had begun in his research. I'm sure Doctor Guillon would have wished his work to be continued and perfected."

Marc could barely control himself. He couldn't believe the man's hypocrisy! "You know very well," he said in a low voice, "that my uncle wanted to put an end to his research. He was afraid the kappa waves would be abused."

"Come now. The doctor was burnt out, depressed from overwork. He saw everything in a negative light. He was making a big fuss over nothing. I'm sure that after a month's vacation, he would have relaxed and started his work again quite willingly."

Regnier's sugary manner while he mouthed these lies was infuriating. Marc clenched his fists in anger, remarking dryly, "My uncle knew exactly what he was doing. He would never have gone back on his decision!"

"The good doctor had his stubborn side, as all old men do. He wasn't himself when he destroyed his equipment. You are much more reasonable, young man. We're counting on you to take up where he left off and complete his research."

Marc couldn't believe Regnier would dare make such an offer. "You've got a lot of gall even to consider such a thing," he exclaimed. "First you caused my uncle's death; now you want me to do something he flatly refused to do!"

Regnier feigned surprise, shaking his head in protest. "You know perfectly well the doctor had a weak heart. The heart attack was inevitable. We kept offering him vacation time but he always refused."

Marc kept silent. He had no evidence to back his claims, and Regnier would never admit to having caused the death of Doctor Guillon. The Director continued: "Understand this, Marc. The research your uncle was doing is very important. You have an obligation to continue it."

The other man shifted in his seat and chose this moment to intervene. "Do it for the good of the nation. You wouldn't want a foreign power to perfect the kappa wave theory before us and use it for dubious purposes, would you?"

"All you want," answered the boy, "is to be the first to 'use it for dubious purposes.'"

An embarrassed silence followed. Then Regnier introduced the man sitting in the back seat. "This is major Ben Gagnon from the Defence Department. His job is to protect Doctor Guillon's discoveries and to make sure they don't fall into the wrong hands."

Marc wondered if the officer was the same man who had accompanied Regnier to his uncle's laboratory on Monday afternoon. In that case, he too would be responsible for Doctor Guillon's death. Marc was sitting with the two men who had murdered the person he had loved most in life.

"The only 'wrong hands' around here," the boy retorted in hatred and rebellion, "are your own."

The Major was a burly man with a square face, hard features and a brush cut. Marc was startled to feel his hand grab the back of his neck. In the rear-view mirror he saw that the officer's face was angry.

"Listen, boy," he said in a stern voice, "You're a citizen and you owe your country a duty of allegiance. The government financed the kappa wave studies, and the government has rights over Doctor Guillon's invention! You're going to tell us where he hid his research notes. They belong to us and we intend to get them back."

Suddenly, Marc lost patience. "My uncle burned his notes! Nothing more exists! And in any case, they never belonged to anyone but him!"

"You're lying," Gagnon said, tightening his grip. "I'm sure he made copies. And if they were destroyed, you're going to help us put the system together again. I know you've got the ability. You're very smart, or so I've heard, and your uncle explained his work to you."

"Never!" Marc cried angrily. He pushed away the major's hand and leaped out of the car on the driver's side, slamming the door behind him. The Major didn't dare stop him because two cemetery workers were passing by as Marc made his escape.

His parents were waiting in their car a few meters away. He joined them and sank down into the back seat without saying a word.

His father inquired, "I hope you accepted the offer Director Regnier made?"

"Not you too!" cried the boy.

"I'm only thinking of your career. They're offering you a high-tech lab, technicians, research assistants at your beck and call, and the opportunity to work with a renowned group of scientists. You didn't refuse him, I hope."

"I won't be bribed."

"You refused!" Mr. Alix thundered. "A salary higher than anyone in your class will see for at least ten years!"

"You want me off your hands, is that it?"

Marc's stepmother couldn't stay neutral after a remark like that. She defended her husband. "You ungrateful little brat! Accusing your father of selfishness when he's only trying to help you and plan your future...."

Marc didn't stay around to hear the end of this tirade. He got out of the car, slammed the door and left the cemetery alone, on foot.

* * *

It was a warm and beautiful day. The snow was melting, exposing patches of grass. Marc wasn't sure where he was going, but he knew he couldn't go home just yet. He wandered to the far end of the cemetery through a gate in the fence, then found himself on the University of Montreal campus near the ski slope and athletic complex. He climbed to the top of the hill and looked out distractedly over the panorama of the north and west sides of the city.

He was both angry and discouraged. Angry at Regnier, who hadn't had the decency to wait with his insulting offers. Angry at Major Gagnon, who spoke deceitfully of the threat of "foreign powers," when all he really wanted was the doctor's notes. And last but not least, angry at his parents who meddled in his affairs without knowing anything of the situation. Even if they had known the truth, Marc doubted whether they would have supported him.

He was discouraged too. It seemed the whole world was against him. He felt utterly alone and vulnerable. He couldn't imagine how he'd get out of the mess he was in.

"All dressed up today, friend!"

Marc started and looked around to see who had spoken. It was Carl Andersen, who had noted the dark suit Marc was wearing for his uncle's funeral.

"Where have you been, all dressed up like that?"

Then Carl noticed how serious Marc looked and his smile disappeared.

"Things not going so well, friend?" he asked, sitting down on the grass beside the boy.

"My uncle died on Monday. We just buried him," Marc said.

"Oh, I'm sorry. Please accept my condolences."

Carl reached out and put his hand gently

41

on Marc's shoulder. "You were very fond of your uncle, weren't you?" he asked softly.

Marc nodded. His throat tightened painfully and tears blurred his vision. He realised sadly that this was the first time since his uncle's death that anyone had shown sincere feeling for him. In a voice choked with emotion he said, "Sometimes I think I'd like to be anywhere else but here."

"You mean anywhere but on this planet?" Carl asked.

The boy nodded. "As far as possible from Earthlings."

Side by side, they sat in the shared silence.

Chapter Four
A Light in the Dark

On Thursday afternoon, the day of the funeral, Marc decided to attend class. He needed distraction and didn't want to dwell on thoughts of death anymore. After his lecture he spent an hour reading in the library.

When he went to his locker to retrieve his coat before leaving, he noticed a small plastic package on the top shelf. It was about the size of a tea bag, filled with white powder. Marc picked it up mechanically, wondering how it had gotten there. It looked like cocaine or some other drug, but who had opened Marc's locker to place it there?

Just then, he felt a hand grab his shoulder, and a deep voice said, "Possession of heroin for purposes of trafficking. You're in deep trouble. Especially with the quantity you've got here."

Marc jumped and turned to face his accuser. The man was large and husky with greying hair. He was dressed in a trenchcoat and looked like a policeman. With him was a much younger man who could have passed for a student — but somehow Marc knew he wasn't one.

Marc threw the bag to the ground, protesting, "It's a frame-up! I've never seen this bag before!"

"What's it doing in your locker then?" asked the older man while the younger one gingerly picked up the package.

"Someone put it there. It's a prank."

"We only know what we see. You'd better come with us."

The officer barely gave him time to take his coat and close his locker. Keeping a firm hand on Marc's shoulder he guided him from the locker area.

"Let me go!" he objected. "Who are you, anyway?"

"Royal Canadian Mounted Police."

The officer flashed a card showing a police badge and identity card. Marc barely had time to read the name: Prevost. The officer released his grip on Marc's shoulder but the two men walked close by him, pushing and hurrying him along.

Marc was intimidated, and even frightened by the men. Would they put him in jail? He had no proof of his innocence. He continued to defend himself, speaking in a low voice to avoid attracting attention.

"I swear to you, someone put it there to frame me!"

But the RCMP officer wasn't listening. "Trafficking heroin is a serious offence. You know how many years in prison it'll get you?"

They left through the eastern exit and walked towards the parking lot. Marc was steered to a car in which a man sat waiting in the back seat. Marc was pushed inside. The youngest officer stayed outside, leaning against the door, while his superior slid into the driver's seat.

Marc recognised the man sitting behind him: Major Ben Gagnon of the Canadian Armed Forces. It was then that he realised the drugs were truly part of a deliberate set-up.

"So it's you!" Marc exclaimed. "Why are you doing this?"

"Simple," said the officer in a cynical tone. "If you refuse to cooperate now, we'll throw you in prison. And for a nice long while, too."

"But you've got no evidence!"

"Evidence has a way of materialising when you need it, as you've just seen. Witnesses too."

"It won't work! There'll be a trial. I'll expose you!"

Gagnon's voice dropped to a menacing hiss. "Who said anything about a trial? Maybe there's a much simpler solution."

He leaned towards Marc and took his knee in an iron grip. The boy winced with pain.

"One day," the Major said in a sinister tone, "you might simply disappear. People would think you had run away. It happens all the time with teenagers. You'd turn up eventually, of course. In the little psychiatric clinic connected to the Armed Forces. Or maybe in the secret military camp we have in the District of Keewatin."

Marc said nothing. He was very afraid. All along he'd suspected that such things went on, but this time they were happening to him. The two men — the Major and the cop — weren't fooling around. They'd had Marc followed for several days now, and they'd broken into his home illegally and searched his room. This evening they were showing him that they'd stop at nothing to get what they were after.

"You know what we want. You're the only person living who knows Doctor Guillon's work, and we're convinced that you've got his research notes."

"I swear I don't have them!" the boy protested.

"Liar!" Gagnon snarled, tightening his grip on Marc's knee. "You're his godson. He confided in you, allowed you to work alongside him. He had no other close associates. You were with him when he destroyed the equipment."

"Go ahead, torture me!" the boy shouted defiantly. "It's right up your alley!"

"Drugs would damage your brain, which everyone says is so precious. But if you don't change your mind by tomorrow morning, we may have to take you for a ride, just to show you we're serious."

To reinforce his point, the major took hold of Marc's hair in his free hand, pulling it until the boy gasped. Marc grabbed his wrist, but the man's grip was too powerful for him.

Finally Gagnon let Marc go and tried to reason with him. "Listen, Marc. The documents in your possession are crucial to the security of this country. If they ever fell into the wrong hands, into foreign hands...."

"The wrong hands!" Marc cried. His eyes were stinging with tears. "You're telling me your hands are clean? These foreign powers that you're so worried about — they're no worse than you are! And anyway, who says you're not working for the CIA yourself?"

"You little brat!" shouted the Major.

And he slapped him hard in the face. Marc was sure the two men were going to beat him up, and he looked desperately for a way to escape. But his captors weren't trying to hold him. Gagnon said simply, "You've got twelve hours to come to your senses. Tomorrow morning we're coming to get you."

Officer Prevost signalled to the third man, still leaning on the door, to stand clear and let Marc out. Marc jumped from the car and sprinted wildly across the parking lot.

* * *

Marc soon had to slow down because of his heart. But he walked as quickly as he could to the esplanade in front of the University's main building. He still had his briefcase in one hand and his coat in the other. He sank down on a bench to catch his breath and threw the coat around his shoulders. His heart galloped alarmingly, and the knowledge of his own approaching death came back to him in a haunting rush.

Marc had no intention of giving into Major Gagnon's blackmail. On the other hand, he was only fifteen and alone in this fight. How could he take on organisations as powerful as the Armed Forces and the RCMP? It was obvious they'd keep up their surveillance until the next morning.

"Good evening, friend. You've worked up quite a sweat."

It was Carl, of course. He was walking on the terrace, enjoying the serenity of the sunset hour. It was uncanny how he always managed to appear just when Marc was most in need of comfort. The young man sat down beside Marc on the cool concrete bench.

The sun, a glowing red disc in a limpid sky, was sinking towards the horizon. The neon lights of Montreal began to twinkle in the gathering darkness.

Carl asked, "This morning you said you dreamed of leaving this planet. Are Earthlings really causing you such trouble?"

Marc nodded silently. If only it were

possible, he'd gladly leave the cruel society of humans, with their police and armed forces.

"You were serious, then?" the young man asked. "I mean, you'd be prepared to leave your parents and friends?"

"I have no friends. None except you, that is. My father wouldn't shed too many tears. We were never all that close. As for my stepmother, I won't go into it."

There was a long silence. Marc's heart was beating more easily now and his breath was even and calm. He got up to go, but Carl held him back.

"What if I offered you a chance to leave this planet? Would you take it?"

Marc managed to smile, even though he didn't really feel like joking. "Sure," he said, "when do we leave?"

"Tonight, if you like."

What a poker face Carl had! He looked so earnest, you'd almost think he was serious.

"Of course," Carl said, "you don't believe a word I said. So here's a question for you. Just where do you think I come from?"

Where did he come from, anyway? Marc had never asked and Carl rarely talked about himself. Intrigued, Marc answered, "I have no idea.... With a name like Andersen, maybe Scandinavia?"

The young man smiled briefly and answered, "Between the orbits of Mars and Jupiter lies the asteroid belt, a zone full of rocks; the largest are like miniature planets. One of these asteroids has been named Erymede. That's where I was born."

The young man seemed so earnest that Marc didn't dare laugh. Besides, Carl's words brought back details of the dream Marc had had the night before. He dimly remembered ships, a voyage through outer space.

"Erymede," the young man continued, "is the home of a human society roughly fifty years more advanced than your own. They call themselves Erymeans and live in underground cities."

Marc sat stock still, watching the young man who claimed to have been born in a place beyond Mars. He looked pretty ordinary for such fantastic origins.

"One aspect of their work is to watch over Earth's people, to prevent a world war or nuclear confrontation. They spy on armies and governments the world over and, through their satellites, they pick up just about everything that's happening here."

The words were like an echo of the boy's dream. They awoke details, clear images in his mind. Marc added, without prompting, "They also have an underground base on the dark side of the moon."

Carl nodded and said, "Correct. I see you've received my transmissions."

"What are you talking about?" Marc asked.

"The dreams you've been having recently...."

"How do you know?"

"I sent those visons to you from a van parked near your house. I have all kinds of devices to transmit holographic images and subliminal waves. The waves induce a state of hypnosis and make it possible to relay messages directly to your brain."

"It can't be!" Marc blurted out. "How long have you been sending me these visions?"

"Ever since I began suspecting that you'd be interested in my proposal."

The boy found himself accepting Carl's story. He himself had worked on kappa waves and their capacity to influence the brain. He knew such things were entirely possible. But this was exactly the kind of long-distance manipulation that Doctor Guillon had feared. He'd stopped his work so that it wouldn't be used to influence unsuspecting people. Marc was impressed, but also a little angry.

"What you're doing — influencing people's thoughts without their consent — that's not very ethical."

"Let me correct you, friend. I sent you certain visions and information so that you might know that Erymeans exist, and that they watch the Earth. I was preparing you so you wouldn't be bowled over when I confronted you in person. My subliminal messages in no way affected your choice or your ability to make a decision. The messages didn't induce you to think or behave in any given way. The desire to leave earth came from within you. I didn't impose it on you. All I've done is suggest that it is possible to leave. You're perfectly free to refuse, to walk away without listening to another word I say."

Marc was reassured by Carl's argument. But he was still having trouble accepting his story. It was all so fantastic, so extraordinary. "Evidence. I need evidence," he said finally.

"What kind of evidence?"

The boy reflected for a moment. If only it could all be true! "I want to see....a ship, a space ship."

"You can't see them from here. They're too far away. But I can arrange for one to send you a signal."

"A signal! Yes, that would do!"

"Pick a spot in the sky."

Marc looked at Carl in disbelief. Then he pointed arbitrarily up at a spot in the heavens. Carl took a rectangular object about the size of a lighter from his pocket. He released a small cursor, then pushed a button and spoke into the apparatus. He was speaking in a language Marc couldn't identify: a bizarre kind of English with French and German mixed in, as well as words of a completely unknown origin.

Then he told Marc, "The cruiser will place itself in geostatic orbit forty degrees above the horizon, due north of Montreal. It will take some time."

Taking his eyes off the device in Carl's hand, Marc looked towards the sky in the direc-

52

tion Carl had indicated. He felt like an idiot. The whole thing was probably a hoax, and Carl would soon laugh right in his face. And yet, what if it was true? Marc noticed that his body was tense, that his hands were trembling. He had completely forgotten Major Gagnon and his threats.

Carl explained, "When our vessels move about in terrestrial orbit, a luminous phenomenon is created which is especially visible at night. We can't do anything about it. People spot these lights in the night and report them as UFOs. In reality, most of them are just our ships."

"You think that UFO I saw two years ago...?"

"Very likely."

Marc blinked anxiously. He thought he'd seen a flash of light, like the momentary streak of a shooting star, but he must have been mistaken. He was so eager for a sign that his imagination was probably playing tricks on him.

A faint voice came out of the miniature transmitter and Carl announced, "Whenever you're ready."

"Go ahead," murmured Marc.

Carl uttered one word, and in the crystalline sky a tiny star gleamed suddenly, flashing three times in two heartbeats, then vanished.

Marc stood transfixed. A great shudder ran through him, from the very base of his spine up to his scalp.

Chapter Five
An Escapade

Silently, Marc scanned the sky for a long time, awaiting further signals, but his efforts were in vain. Carl had replaced the transmitter in his pocket. He was quiet, knowing that Marc would be filled with conflicting emotions.

At last Marc shook himself and asked, "They are humans, you said. How did they ever end up on an asteroid?"

"They lived for many generations in an underground city in Siberia, but at the beginning of the century they decided to leave Earth. For some years they lived on the Moon, but for two generations now they've been on Erymede."

"What role do I play in all this? Why do I get an invitation to join the Erymeans?"

"At the end of the eighteenth century, the ancestors of the Erymeans were chosen from among the most gifted men and women of their generation. They didn't have to be well-known scholars and philosophers. Since that time, we have kept up the tradition of recruiting from among talented people on Earth. Today, scientists are joining us because they want to contribute to our mission."

"That explains many disappearances," said Marc. "When Western scientists vanish, we always say they've defected to the East. When they disappear in the East, people say they've fled West."

"Exactly. The majority of great scientists suspected of treason have ended up with us. So Erymede acquires more human resources. But we try to attract mainly young people like you with exceptional abilities. We figure your talents will be more effectively used on Erymede than on Earth. At your age people are more likely to be attracted by the adventure of shipping off into the unknown."

"So you're a sort of recruiting officer?"

"A few dozen of us work in the universities and at scientific congresses and similar events. For the time being I'm responsible for eastern Canada."

"But what would I be expected to do on Erymede?"

"Well, first of all, you'd receive scientific and technical education in an area that interests you. You'd be studying with boys and girls your age who have more or less the same level of knowledge as you."

"They'd be my age?"

"Sure! Not that every young Erymean is a child genius, but our educational methods are very advanced. We teach our young people

55

primarily by hypnopedagogy. It's a lot faster than traditional techniques."

"Hypnopedagogy?"

"Instruction by hypnosis. We transmit knowledge directly to the brain. At twenty years old, young Erymeans have the equivalent of one or two of your university Ph.Ds."

Marc could hardly believe it. So that was how the Erymeans had become so advanced! Everyone was an accomplished scholar at twenty, and learning was a relatively painless process.

"Here's my offer," said Carl. "Tonight, I'll take you for a little visit to Argus, our lunar base. We'll be back before dawn. If you're still interested after seeing Argus, I'll give you several days to think over your decision. If you decide it's not for you, I'll erase all memory of the voyage, and you'll wake up tomorrow without the faintest recollection of these events."

"You can induce amnesia?"

"It's easy. We have a special drug whose dosage determines the period of time erased. We can even create false memories with hypnosis to fill in the gap of time unaccounted for. We need this mechanism to guard the secret of our existence."

"But how will we get there?"

"By shuttle. Our regional base for all north eastern America is in the state of Maine."

Marc hesitated, checking for the agent who was never far behind him. Finally, he spotted the familiar car parked among the others in front of the University's main building. It was the same one that had parked in front of his house the night before. He could see two figures, but they were too far off for him to make out their features. He was certain they were agents of the RCMP.

"The location of our regional base is a closely guarded secret," Carl said. "We'll have to shake off your friends from the police."

Marc looked up in utter surprise.

"How do you know about it?" he asked.

"I tuned in on your arrest. I managed to follow your discussions with the help of a small ultrasensitive directional microphone."

"But the car windows were shut!"

"Glass isn't concrete. I managed to pick up the essentials of the conversation. And I listened in on what they said after you left. There are three men trailing you. Two of them stay together in the brown Ford. The youngest one is the one who arrested you. Then there's the officer with the greying hair...."

"Prevost."

"He's in his own car — a grey Chevrolet. He's there in case you shake off the other two."

"It'll be hard to shake them."

"Don't you worry about it," Carl replied.

* * *

Officer Prevost sat in his parked car in front of the Polytechnical School. He was communicating with the other two agents by radio.

"The guy he was talking to is leaving," they informed him.

"Which direction?" asked Prevost.

"West."

"Did the boy hand him anything?"

"We didn't see anything. I think he's just a student, a friend who sat down to chat."

"What's Alix up to?"

"He's still sitting there."

About five minutes later one of the agents announced, "Alix is leaving. Heading west."

"Trail him as closely as you can without letting him know you're there. Don't lose sight of him. I'll be right behind you."

Prevost started the engine and took the campus road that went down towards the main building and Edouard-Montpetit Boulevard. He had just turned onto the esplanade in front of the main building when the other agents' voices filled the car.

"He just boarded a car that was parked at the end ..."

The second agent interrupted, "It's the guy he was talking to,the...."

The receiver went dead. Prevost spotted the brown Ford, stopped on the other side of the esplanade. What was going on?

Only one car, a green Volkswagen Rabbit, was coming from the other direction, but there weren't any passengers inside. The car with Marc Alix in it must have gone the other way.

As Officer Prevost watched the vehicle pass, he felt his own car suddenly stall. The Rabbit, meanwhile, continued at a good clip while Prevost tried in vain to restart the engine. Nothing happened. The battery seemed completely dead.

Just then he noticed his two agents standing next to their own stationary vehicle, waving madly. Officer Prevost realised too late that the Rabbit must have been carrying the Alix boy. He pushed open his car door and ran to the edge of the terrace overlooking the campus. He was just in time to see the little green car disappearing east along Edouard Montpetit Boulevard.

*   *   *

Marc sat up from his hiding place behind the front seat and stared in open curiosity at a fixture on the Rabbit's ceiling. It was a grey box, rectangular and flat. One side featured what looked like the front part of a camera, only there was no lens.

This device, which pivoted on an axis and could tilt upwards, was controlled by a small box Carl had placed between the front seats. There were several switches, a few lights and a small monitor. This was the device that had short-circuited the cars of the RCMP agents.

"How does this thing work?" Marc asked.

"It would take a while to explain. Basically, it emits a neutralising wave pattern that inhibits current in an electrical circuit. It'll drain a car battery instantaneously. You'll have all the time you want to get acquainted with our gadgets later."

The Rabbit turned north at the first street and proceeded quickly along Wilderton Avenue to the railway tracks separating the Cote des Neiges district from the Town of Mount Royal.

The south side of the road bordering these tracks was lined with factories and warehouses. Carl slowed down beside a nondescript building and flipped a switch on the dashboard. The building's garage door opened and the Rabbit ducked inside.

Moments later a helicopter lifted off from a pad in the rear courtyard of the warehouse.

"What efficiency!" Marc exclaimed as they flew over the summit of Mount Royal. It was his first trip in a helicopter. He'd never suspected they flew so fast. He asked, "The mechanic who helped us on board is Erymean, right?"

"No. Most of our collaborators and informers have no idea where we're from. Usually we tell them we're working with the United Nations secret service."

"But there's no such thing!"

"That proves how secret it is!" Carl told

him, laughing.

The helicopter had been airborne only five minutes, but already Mount Saint Bruno was falling behind, to the left.

"What speed are we flying at?" Marc exclaimed.

"We tinkered with this helicopter a bit. We replaced the turbine engine with a miniature reactor. We're cruising at about three hundred kilometres per hour. Do you know Maine at all?"

"Mountains and forests."

"Exactly. Almost the entire population lives in the southern half of the state. Our base is in the west-central sector, near the Quebec border. The closest village is thirty kilometres away."

"What about crossing the border?"

"We'll hedgehop."

The countryside raced by under the helicopter, a black expanse etched with dotted lines of light.

Carl Andersen seemed perfectly at ease as a pilot. In the darkness, Marc reckoned they were passing the mountains of Quebec's Eastern Townships region. The ridges seemed alarmingly high, but the helicopter wove its way effortlessly between them with the help of its radar. About halfway to their destination they saw an expanse of glittering lights: the city of Sherbrooke. Then the forest turned dense and black, and they hardly saw another light until they landed. The young pilot made radio contact with the base while they were still in flight and murmured a few words of Erymean — a language that was both foreign and strangely familiar to Marc's ear.

When Carl announced that they'd be landing soon, nothing in the terrain below gave the slightest hint that there was a base nearby. As the helicopter slowed, a clutch of blue lights lit up, laid out in a broad letter "H". The landing pad was in a dark valley near a small lake, whose waters reflected the Moon's scattered beams.

The helicopter dropped to a gentle landing. The moment it touched down, Marc noticed other lights, all shaded so as not to be visible from above. As he stepped onto the pad he made out a hangar, probably reserved for the helicopter, an elegant little chalet, and a two-car garage.

"Is this the regional base?" Marc asked dubiously.

"This is all Earthlings get a chance to see. The base is underground, of course."

A mechanic approached them, pushing a small tractor to tow the helicopter into the hangar. Aside from him, the place seemed deserted.

Carl and the mechanic spoke briefly in Erymean. Marc, whose ear was becoming accustomed to the language, gathered that they were talking about the garage. Marc asked if the base was protected against intruders.

"The entire perimeter of the base," Carl told him, "is guarded by an elaborate detection system. We have heat detectors, seismographs buried in the soil, infra-red and regular cameras, microphones and long-distance radar. Every inbound aircraft is monitored, as is any ground vehicle that happens to roll onto one of the two dirt roads lead here. If hikers stumble onto the property, their body heat gives them away, along with the vibrations of their footsteps. We track them as long as they remain near the compound."

As Carl went on with his explanation, the mechanic finished rolling the helicopter into the hangar. Carl and Marc followed him and the huge door clanged shut behind them. The entire floor of the hangar then sank into the ground, much like the elevator on an aircraft carrier. They descended rapidly and Marc found himself in the middle of an immense hall with dozens of helicopters lined up in two rows.

Carl explained, "This base serves all Erymean agents working in south eastern Canada and the north eastern United States, from Detroit to Saint John's, from Sept-Iles to Washington D.C."

They left the mechanic and turned right, crossing a parking lot with several cars. The floor of the garage next to the chalet doubled as a car elevator, just as the hangar floor doubled as one for helicopters.

"I won't give you a tour of this base," Carl

told him, "because there's so much more to see on the Moon. But it might interest you to know that the lower floors here contain computers that receive all the information collected in this region. They collate it and beam it up to Argus. We get our information from newspapers, wire services, magazines and the broadcast media. It's all collected locally, then sent to the base. Every day we comb publications like the New York Times and the Washington Post, not to mention the thousands of news broadcasts aired every day on networks like the CBC and NBC. The same thing goes on in every part of the world. Whether it's politics, economics, science, or culture, nothing escapes Argus."

A door in front of them opened to reveal a second cavernous hangar. But the vehicles inside were of another kind altogether. At first glance, they looked like a fleet of flying saucers. But Marc noticed that they weren't really saucer-shaped at all. Their corners had been rounded and their sides were slightly convex, but their general shape was rectangular. The outside of these vehicles was unremarkable, and certainly no one would have called them sleek. Comparable to fair-sized trailers in size, they were all of a drab grey colour that seemed to vary slightly with the particular surroundings of each vehicle.

"These are the shuttles," Carl said. "They're used to transport passengers between Earth and the Moon, or between Earth and the orbiting cruisers."

The hangar was empty. While Marc examined the strange vehicles, Carl went to an intercom attached to the wall and asked which shuttle they could use. A green light began to blink above one of the vehicles and the two young men walked in its direction.

The shuttles rested on four squat legs. Boarding was done at the back, where a retractable gangway emerged from under a sliding door. To the right of the airlock, inside the door, was a baggage hold. The cabin itself contained four rows of three seats for passengers, and two seats up front for the pilot and co-pilot.

The shuttle's interior was dark. A dim glow came through the broad pilot's window in front, just above the instrument panel. Carl guided Marc to the co-pilot's seat and told him to fasten his shoulder harness. He whispered a command and the whole console came to life: monitors, instrument lights, and an array of switches and cursors. Marc was surrounded by this dizzying display of technology.

With all this instrumentation before him, Marc assumed that take-off would be a complicated affair. As it turned out, the pilot had the option of relegating take-off control to the on-board computer. The shuttle was pulled along rails embedded in the hangar floor to the launch area. This was a vast hall separated from the hangar space by a sliding door. A huge retractable panel slid open above them and Marc found himself gazing up into a rectangle of starry night.

"Behind the chalet," Carl said, "a gentle slope leads to the lake. Near the top of this slope, beside the house, there's an old clay tennis court. That's the rectangle you're looking through right now."

Carl typed their destination code into the on-board computer's keyboard. Their course map flashed before them on the computer screen. Carl glanced at it, then put the shuttle on automatic pilot. After this, there was virtually nothing left to do. Commands were given directly by the computer, with the monitor registering each manoeuvre as it was executed.

The shuttle vibrated slightly as it rose towards the hole in the roof of the launch area, and in a moment it was through. Carl activated one of the shuttle's video cameras and pointed it Earthward, and the lighted windows of the chalet appeared on a screen just in front of Marc. He watched the chalet grow rapidly smaller as the tennis court rolled back to cover the glowing blue rectangle of the launching pad. Soon not even the lake was visible.

The extreme rate of acceleration pressed Marc back into his seat, but he felt no ill effects. The shuttle was equipped with a system designed to compensate for the crushing forces of acceleration. The system would maintain a comfortable level of artificial gravity throughout the flight.

But Marc hardly had time to ponder this kind of detail. There was only one thought in his mind now: he was going to the Moon!

Chapter Six
Arbiters of the Earth

Already the coast of Maine was visible in distance, indented with bays and inlets. The ocean glimmered distantly in the Moonlight. To starboard, just ahead of them, Marc made out a Boeing 747 going in the same direction as the shuttle, but much more slowly.

"Won't they see us?" he asked.

"The shuttle is equipped with anti-radar and optical screens. The same is true of our space ships in orbit around Earth."

"What are optical screens?"

"They're supposed to make the ship invisible. They were developed only a few years ago. Before that, when we were spotted, people took our shuttles for UFOs. Our old model was responsible for the term 'flying saucers.'"

"So those 'flying saucers' were really your shuttles?"

"Most of them. Now we have optical screens, but the system still needs to be perfected. Our vehicles are often spotted as lights glimmering in the night, or as luminous reflections by day. Then there's the exhaust from our reactors and retrothrusters. It all depends on the vantage point of the observer, the air density, humidity and atmospheric ionisation."

Marc thought back to the UFO he'd seen two years ago in the Lake Megantic area. It had disappeared somewhere over Maine. He knew now it had been an Erymean shuttle making its way to the regional base.

The little ship was steadily gaining altitude and speed. The jetliner had been left behind long ago. To the east, the sky was lightening rapidly. It looked like a sunrise in time-lapse photography. Marc pointed to a luminous point moving at a very high altitude.

"Is that an artificial satellite?" he asked.

"Yes. The sky is full of them. Meteorological satellites, telecommunications satellites, others designed for exploration or strategic observation. Every time an Earth nation launches one of those things, we intercept it in orbit and install a little pirating device so that Argus receives the information it collects and the messages it sends. We call this 'parasiting' off a satellite. That makes our surveillance work much simpler: Earthlings unwittingly provide us with the tools for it. For instance, let's say an American spy satellite picks up troop movements in China. Argus knows about it the moment Washington finds out."

The sun blazed over the horizon, lighting up cloud banks below the shuttle and causing the glittering stars to fade. The curvature of the Earth became clearly visible. Through gaps in the clouds, Marc made out the contours of Scandinavia.

He was awestruck by the magnificent view unfolding below him. The sun, filtered by the shuttle's window, burned brilliantly in the deep blue sky. Soon the Earth was no longer visible through the window, as the shuttle's course turned directly away from the planet. Carl activated the stern camera, and the Earth's surface surged onto the video screen, a swirl of ragged white clouds through which the oceans' deep blue and the green and brown outlines of the continents could be seen.

Marc was marvelling at a sight that only a handful of Earth astronauts had ever seen. He had never dreamed that someday he might travel in space himself, yet here he was, after a very unexpected chain of events. Two hours ago, he had been on Earth, caught in a sordid tangle of greed and cruelty. Now he was sitting in the co-pilot's seat of a spacecraft. The cabin was spacious and comfortable, suffused with a soft pink light. The lights on the instrument panel formed ever-changing patterns while words and charts appeared and faded silently on a bank of monitors.

This experience was far different from the reports of NASA flights. Here, the computer did everything. The pilot might just as well sleep for the entire flight. In the upholstered comfort of the cabin it was difficult to imagine the frozen airless environment outside.

The radar screen indicated the presence of a distant object. Carl read the information offered by the computer, then issued a command for a visual image on the video screen. A man-made satellite came up on the screen. It was a large machine, bristling with antennae. The Erymean explained, "It's one of Argus' satellite relay stations. We don't limit ourselves to parasiting Earth-made satellites. We also have spy satellites of our own. They pick up most communication by Hertzian wave. They aren't sensitive enough for radio traffic like taxi dispatch systems or ham radio gossip, but they do pick up all the powerful and important signals, like communications between a country and its embassies abroad, or between a nation's ships and their headquarters. The ultrasensitive antennae you see on the satellite pick up signals and relay them to Argus, where computers sort and classify the information."

Carl paused for a moment, then added, "Now you know all there is to know about our surveillance and information network, from the regional bases to the Earth satellite parasiting devices to our own relay stations. The brain of this network is located on the far side of the Moon, at Argus."

The entire planet Earth was now visible on the video screen, partly in the dark. A new signal appeared on the radar monitor. Carl explained that the craft's "radar" was actually an apparatus called a "viseptor," vastly more powerful and precise than conventional radar.

"Here's something that might interest you," Carl said, peering at the signal on the monitor. "Let's make a little detour so you can see it up close."

Using the shuttle's computer, he charted a shallow curve in the craft's course, then punched it in. The automatic pilot responded accordingly. "Watch carefully," he warned. "We'll be passing at terrific speed."

He pointed out the window at a pale spot that seemed to be growing fast before them. Marc had a fleeting glimpse of an immense ship as the shuttle sped beneath it. It was a space ship of impressive size, a cruiser as big as a destroyer, with bulky projections.

"Cruisers are our most formidable ships," Carl commented. "There are now six of them in orbit around Earth. In peacetime, their mission is to intercept ground-launched satellites and install the parasite transmitters I told you about. In a period of war, if one superpower launched a missile attack against an enemy nation, the cruisers would act to neutralise the missiles' nuclear warheads. Similarly, they'd intervene to paralyse a squadron of bombers or a missile-carrying submarine fleet. They'd do this with neutraliser beams that block the electronic guidance and detonation systems. If outright destruction of the missiles or bombers became

71

necessary, the cruisers would use their banks of laser cannon — believe me, those are precise and powerful. And if it ever happened that the cruisers were overwhelmed, even momentarily, each would launch three interceptors, which can be sent into the atmosphere in pursuit of air squadrons or nuclear submarines."

The cruiser they'd just passed was now a tiny, fading point on the viseptor screen. Carl continued, "Of course, this means that world war is no longer possible. We would step in immediately to prevent bombardments. Up until now, we've allowed certain regional conflicts to continue, like the wars in south-east Asia and the Middle East, because we don't want to reveal our existence yet. But the day may come when we're forced to intervene openly. On that day, Earthlings will meet their arbiters."

Marc stared at Carl in surprise. He was beginning to discover the young man's true personality. Carl wasn't just a gentle dreamer talking in abstract terms about peace and non-aggression. He represented a formidable power that kept watch over the Earth, ready to reveal itself to Earthlings if and when the need should arise.

* * *

In two hours, the shuttle managed a journey that had taken the Apollo missions four days to accomplish. Marc watched as the white crescent loomed ever larger. As they approached, he began to make out details of the Moon's surface. The milky whiteness of Earth's natural satellite became tinged with tan and grey.

Carl was quiet. He felt he'd said enough for the moment. Marc had a lifetime ahead of him to discover Erymede if he chose to leave Earth.

In the silence of the cabin, Marc thought about all the implications of the events he was experiencing. He had always been pessimistic about the future. He was convinced that one day a world war would break out and the nations of the world would annihilate each other with their arsenals of nuclear, chemical and biological weapons. In the 1970s, people had taken refuge in a false sense of security, but today, things were different. Energy was ever more scarce as conventional fuels dwindled, and hunger was a crushing reality throughout the developing world. These problems raised the stakes high enough to provoke serious conflict and justify the use of weapons that could wipe out humanity.

But now Marc knew about Argus and the Erymeans. He found himself willing to believe in the future again. World war could be averted. Marc had often wondered about the use of embarking on a scientific career, especially since Doctor Guillon had opened his eyes to the political manipulation of science. Marc had wondered if there was anyone he could work for in good conscience, and had shuddered to think that his efforts might eventually yield rewards to one or another of the world's armies. He had not thought it better to work for the multinational corporations, whose insatiable hunger for natural resources and cold disregard for the environment repelled him. So the choices were limited, even though many opportunities would be offered to such a talented youth.

But now he was being offered a chance to work in an organisation dedicated to protecting Earth's inhabitants from their own madness. It was a chance to leave behind the sordid realities of the world and to become a voyager in space, something he'd never thought possible, though he was born in the Apollo era.

Landing preparations disturbed Marc from his reveries. The Moon was now directly before them. It looked like a giant balloon floating just above the shuttle. Much of it was in shadow, but even so, Marc was able to pick out surface contours highlighted in dark grey and black.

"The Argus base," Carl explained, "is located inside the eastern cliffs of the great Tsiolkovsky Crater. This crater is on the side of the Moon that's always hidden from Earth."

"What about the unmanned probes that photographed that side of the Moon? Weren't they able to detect the base?"

"Most of our installations are underground. Those that are above ground, like our parabolic antennae, are well camouflaged to blend in with the surrounding environment. They're also fully retractable, in case an Earth probe passes too close."

The main thrusters at the shuttle's stern had been engaged for most of the flight. Now the retrothrusters were engaged. They consisted of three rectangular openings under the shuttle's bow which emitted an intense white glow, though less spectacular than the flaming rockets of Earth spacecraft.

The Moon continued to grow before them and soon filled the shuttle's window. The shuttle's automatic pilot executed a slow rotating manoeuvre so that the craft's belly was eventually foremost, in anticipation of touchdown on the lunar surface.

The ground which now raced beneath the shuttle seemed flat, but the Moon was still a study in contrasts: wide areas of impenetrable shadow abutted on regions of brilliant illumination; immense cliffs and plateaus seemed to have been cut from the lunar surface with a cleaver, so abruptly did they rise from the Moonscape.

The shuttle was clearly slowing down now, even though Marc could barely feel the deceleration. Lights flashed busily on the instrument panel, and video screens charted the craft's landing procedures even as the automatic pilot executed them. The vehicle flew over the Tsi-olkovsky Crater, carefully avoiding the mountain that towered at its centre.

Another shuttle appeared in the distance on the opposite side of the crater. It rapidly gained altitude, its silhouette clearly visible against the starry sky. Then it disappeared, heading off to a rendezvous with a cruiser or perhaps to one of the regional bases on Earth.

Nervously, Marc watched the mountains that towered over the crater to the east. They showed steep slopes and sudden cliffs, all dizzyingly high, and Marc was beginning to wonder if the shuttle was going to smash right into them.

Chapter Seven
Argus

"Don't you think you should take over the helm again?" Marc asked anxiously. "We seem to be flying kind of low — and too fast."

Carl Andersen laughed gently. "Everything's all right," he said. "The landing pads are built into the cliffs. We're heading straight for them."

Marc was gripping the sides of his seat as he felt the shuttle slow down, and he was glad that he'd securely fastened his shoulder harness. The shuttle now advanced diagonally at a much slower rate toward the threatening cliffs.

"Look," said Carl, pointing out the window.

He'd spotted a space ship that seemed about to sink into the cliffs. Its long frame resembled that of an ordinary city bus, though it was easily a dozen times as big.

"An astrobus," Carl exclaimed. "Every day it makes the round trip from Argus to Erymede. Most of the people who work on Argus have their permanent homes on Erymede. They go back regularly by astrobus for holidays."

In the mountains just in front of the astrobus, a vast rectangle seemed to pull itself from the cliff, then slide to one side, revealing an enclosure large enough to fit a five-storey building. This was the astrobus landing area, lit up in red.

The Erymean continued, "Erymede is one of the asteroids closest to Earth's orbit. What's more, its speed and trajectory have been modified so that it now follows Earth as it circles the sun. It takes exactly 365.23 days, just like the Earth. Their orbits have been synchronised, and Erymede maintains an average distance of five light minutes, or ninety million kilometres, from Earth. It takes the astrobus about six hours to make the trip."

"Six hours!" Marc exclaimed. "Space probes launched by NASA take sixteen weeks!"

The astrobus gradually descended into the red-lit hall and came to rest on the landing pad. The cliff face slid closed and another rectangle, smaller this time, opened in the rocks to the right and lower down. The shuttle executed a sharp turn and positioned itself in line with the opening.

"There are two pads for shuttles," Carl explained. "One for landings, the other for take-offs."

The vast room where the shuttle touched down was identical to the one Marc had seen on

Earth. But beyond the airlock an entirely different world awaited him.

Apart from their language, with its strange-sounding consonants, the most striking thing about the Erymeans was their small stature. Here on Argus, Carl Andersen was taller than his countrymen, while on Earth he was of average height.

Carl explained that Erymean geneticists had determined the ideal height of their citizens with a view to economy of space in the design of vehicles and architecture. This was important for a people who lived underground, blasting their dwellings out of rock, and it was especially important on Erymede, a tiny planet barely a hundred kilometres in diameter.

Another peculiarity of the Erymeans was the absence of distinct racial identity. Few of them seemed clearly black or white. They seemed to be a mixture of all races, and most had a light-brown complexion, the colour of sun-tanned Caucasians. Physical characteristics varied widely. Carl had blond hair and fair skin, but his eyes were dark and almond-shaped. For five or six generations now, individuals of different races had intermingled on Erymede, where the Earthly notion of nationality didn't exist. The only remaining trace of it could be found in family names. Erymeans had a common language. Those who still learned the many languages of Earth did so to facilitate surveillance, or for personal interest.

The Erymeans lived in almost constant shadow; even their artificial light was subdued. Carl explained that this was done to save energy. They were also accustomed to an ambient temperature of nineteen degrees Celcius, which Marc found uncomfortably cool.

A conservationist philosophy lay behind these measures. In the past, man had taken up too much space and had wasted natural resources in the production of energy he didn't really need. It was becoming increasingly important for people to learn how to economise on space and re-examine their use of natural resources. Had principles of conservation been applied on Earth, the planet wouldn't be in the dire straits it was in today. Overpopulation wouldn't be a problem; food and energy resources would meet the needs of the entire population — this according to Carl, at any rate.

Marc asked, "When will you reveal your existence to Earthlings?"

"That, friend," Carl answered, "is one of the hottest topics of debate on Erymede."

* * *

It would be useless to describe all the wonders Marc encountered in the depths of Argus. The base, which was as large and complex as a city, was built on many levels. The lowest levels descended even deeper into the

Moon than the floor of the Tsiolkovsky Crater itself. In the dim light of its halls and corridors, an entire population went about what seemed to be very active and contented lives, unbeknownst to Earth people, who thought of the Moon as a lifeless desert.

What impressed Marc most was the headquarters of Argus Control. "Argus Control" was the organisation in charge of maintaining Earth surveillance and preventing world war or ecological disaster. All information obtained from Earth sources by local informants, regional bases, satellite "parasites," relay stations and patrol ships eventually found its way here. All political, military, industrial, cultural and scientific activity on Earth — except, perhaps, what went on in people's minds — could be found stored in the memory of the central computer, Argus C.C.

It was possible to enter the very brain of this machine and walk down the long, narrow passages whose cold walls glimmered with patterns of instrument lights. Argus C.C. did not only possess a memory; it possessed intelligence, albeit limited. No human being, not even a team of a thousand scientists, could have analysed the huge quantities of information coming from Earth. For every important item, ten turned out to be trivial. Argus C.C. did the preliminary sorting, weighing each fact according to a complex list of criteria with which Erymean programmers had supplied it. It made comparisons and associations, performed cross-checks and executed billions of complex operations in mere seconds.

In other rooms linked to the main computer by work stations, teams of specialists studied the materials transmitted to them by Argus C.C. They continually consulted the computer's inexhaustible data banks, calling up tables of statistics, probability and trend studies. This information helped them predict with considerable accuracy fluctuations in world markets or the onset of political crises.

Marc was fascinated by the three-storey circular room where the most important Earthly events were transmitted live. On both the ground floor and mezzanine, lining the circular walls, dozens of men and women called "observers" sat before video screens. They were keeping tabs on critical situations on Earth, such as the unfolding of a civil war, the sinking of a super-tanker or the rise and fall of a major currency.

On a raised command platform in the room's centre, members of the Argus Council took turns monitoring events. They followed the unfolding of a crisis on an hourly basis on giant screens which hung from the ceiling. They could ask any analyst or observer for information and receive answers almost immediately on their earphones or monitors.

The highest authority on Argus was the Council, consisting of fifteen members who met on a regular basis to look over observation reports, discuss various situations and decide whether direct intervention was called for. If an urgent crisis arose, the three on-duty councillors in the control room at the critical moment were authorised to make on-the-spot decisions. The commanders of the six cruisers, and of every regional base on Earth, received their orders from the Council.

Much more could be said about the workings of Argus, and Marc would have spent weeks exploring the base without covering everything there was to see. But he had to think about getting back. He wanted to be in Montreal before dawn. His parents were probably beside themselves with worry. Marc was not the type to stay out late, let alone disappear for an entire night. He'd have trouble thinking up a believable excuse. Maybe, he thought to himself, it would be better not to go home at all. He could destroy the hidden microfiches and then take off immediately with Carl.

How would Marc's parents feel if he disappeared forever? His stepmother would, at the very most, be annoyed by the whole thing. Marc didn't really care what she felt. The real question was how his father would take it. Did he love his son more than he let on? If this were true, wouldn't it be cruel to leave without a word of explanation?

On the other hand, he might put the disappearance out of his mind and eventually find some relief in having the boy gone. How was Marc to know? It was quite possible he'd misjudged his father all these years. Perhaps Mr. Alix deserved a lot more affection than he'd received.

But it was too late to sort it all out. It was out of the question for Marc to divulge his plans. Besides, Mr. Alix would probably scoff at the idea of Erymeans scuttling about under the Moon's surface. Marc would have to close the door firmly and for good on his past. The future, which he'd already glimpsed, was more important. Cutting ties with Earth would be easier if he buried his emotional attachments.

* * *

After a two-hour stay that went by all too quickly, Carl and Marc boarded their shuttle in the cool blue light of the launch area. The lights turned red, the huge door slid open, revealing the desolate Moonscape of the Tsiolkovsky Crater and a sky as black as ink. The small craft lifted off gently and began to accelerate.

Marc had made up his mind. A few hours from now, he would leave Earth forever.

Chapter Eight
Marc's Death

The Director's car turned into the driveway and stopped in front of the Freeman Foundation building. Charles Regnier got out. He was in a very bad mood. He stepped up to a car parked directly in front of his own just as Major Ben Gagnon opened the door and got out. Not bothering to hide his annoyance, Regnier asked, "What on Earth is so important that you had to call me away from home? Can't anyone else ever take care of anything?"

"Marc Alix has vanished," the Major said grimly.

"Don't look at me! That's your problem. And the RCMP's."

"Wrong," said the Major. "If the research data on kappa waves gets into foreign hands, you and your colleagues at the Foundation will have to work seven days a week to find out Guillon's secrets."

"Who says the Alix boy defected?"

"No one. But he shook off my men with the help of a student, or at any rate someone posing as a student. I've got a hunch he's a foreign agent who convinced Alix to leave the country."

"Just what do you want me to do?"

"We've got to find where the second set of microfiche is hidden and get there before Marc Alix does. I don't want him leaving the country with that information! I'm convinced his uncle told him where they're hidden the day he destroyed his lab equipment."

"The tape was filled with static, you know that. We both listened to it Monday night. Impossible to make anything out."

"We gave up too easily. This time we'll figure out what the old man said."

Ben Gagnon pointed to a man getting out of his car with three metal cases that looked very heavy.

"This gentleman," said the Major, "is an electronics specialist who works in acoustics and magnetic recordings. If anyone can piece Guillon's words together, he can."

The specialist, whose name was Burrell, took two of the cases, and the Major took one. Regnier led them into the Foundation building and they made their way to the security department.

Leroux, chief of security for the Foundation, arrived within minutes of being summoned by Regnier. He led the group through his office into an adjacent room. Under normal circumstances, only Regnier, Leroux and two assistants were allowed in this room. This was where all the covert taping of conversations was done. Most of the important offices and laboratories were equipped with hidden microphones, which was how Regnier had kept tabs on Doctor Guillon. The old doctor had been right to suspect that something was going on.

The room was filled with electronic equipment, tape recorders and metal cabinets filled with reels of tape. The security chief consulted a computer file, then went to get the particular tape they wanted from the locked cabinet. They played it once while Lieutenant Burrell unpacked his equipment. All that could be heard was a faint crackling that partially drowned out the voices whispering in the background. It was impossible to make out what the doctor was saying to his nephew.

"What's causing the interference?" Major Gagnon asked.

"Doctor Guillon must have had some piece of electronic equipment running in the room where he was speaking," Burrell answered. "Was he in his laboratory?"

"Yes," said Regnier. "There are any number of devices that could have caused the interference."

"The doctor and his companion are almost whispering," Burrell added. "Did they know they were being bugged?"

"It's very possible," Regnier said.

"Well, we'll try to get rid of the interference," Lieutenant Burrell announced.

* * *

It was nearly five o'clock in the morning. Regnier was sleeping in the chief of security's office. Leroux dozed in a chair in the listening room, while Burrell and Gagnon strained for the hundredth time to make out the scratchy, virtually inaudible conversation between Doctor Guillon and Marc Alix.

Major Gagnon wearily summed up, "At least we know that Guillon hid the second series of microfiches and told his nephew where they were. So far we've been able to decipher 'the envelope,' 'left side' and 'twenty centimetres.' But that just isn't enough."

Lieutenant Burrell had successfully eliminated a good part of the crackling. The voices were coming through more clearly, but they were still indistinct and difficult to follow. Every once in a while a word filtered through, and the two men tried to guess the rest of the sentence.

The sound expert listened again and again, tirelessly, to the most crucial segment, hoping his experienced ear would piece together the slurred words.

"Cemetery!" he exclaimed suddenly.

"What?" Gagnon asked.

"The old guy said 'cemetery!'"

He rewound the tape and listened to the segment one more time. Yes, it sounded like 'cemetery'. But how about the word 'neige' they could distinctly make out in the same sentence?

"The Notre-Dame-des-Neiges Cemetery!" Major Gagnon cried. "The envelope with the microfiche is hidden somewhere in the graveyard!"

"It's just a hypothesis," Regnier said when they wakened him and told him of their discovery.

"It's the only clue we have," Gagnon retorted. "Listen, didn't his wife die a few years back?"

"Yes."

"Guillon must attend to her grave once in a while. He could have hidden the envelope somewhere near the tombstone."

"Guillon was buried there yesterday morning. You're not going to dig him up, are you?" Regnier objected.

But the Major was busy thinking aloud. "Remember the burial? Marc Alix stayed beside the grave until everyone else had gone. Maybe he was hoping to get the microfiche out of the hiding place. Maybe he realised it was too risky in broad daylight, so he didn't chance it. He may very well have returned there after shaking off the RCMP agents."

"It's too late, then," Director Regnier sighed. "His uncle told him to destroy the files. You heard it just like I did."

"I'm going to go anyway, just in case. I've got nothing to lose."

* * *

Marc didn't want Carl Andersen to accompany him to the cemetery. He wanted to fulfil his uncle's last wish alone. It would be Marc's last important act on Earth. To Marc, burning the microfiche symbolised his rejection of earthly society, his protest against those who would use science as a means of oppression.

Carl was uneasy about the plan. He didn't want Marc going off alone because he knew the RCMP were still hot on his trail. The boy had asked him to let him off at the University of Montreal athletic complex. He was planning to enter the cemetery from behind the ski hill.

In the Rabbit's rear view mirror, Carl watched Marc disappear towards Vincent d'Indy Street. The boy was taking a big chance. What if the hiding place had been discovered by the RCMP? Maybe they'd known about it for a while and were using it as a trap to catch Marc.

Acting on an impulse, the Erymean took the miniature radio out of his pocket and made contact with the regional base in Maine.

* * *

At the top of the ski hill Marc sank down on the grass. He should have taken an easier route. He was out of breath, his heart beating as if ready to burst. But he had no time to lose. The

90

eastern sky was already growing paler, and soon dawn would begin creeping over Montreal. As his breathing grew steadier, he rose and began to walk toward the cemetery. He got through the fence without much trouble at a point where the wire was ripped open, and once he was inside it didn't take him long to find his bearings. He headed west without losing sight of the fence that bordered the cemetery grounds. His uncle's grave was just about level with the Polytechnical School.

Marc walked quietly down the shadowy paths. The walk was far from enjoyable. Not that he was afraid of ghosts — he had never been the superstitious type. He just didn't want to meet the watchman doing his nightly rounds. Besides, the setting was undeniably sinister. The moon still gleamed above him, throwing strange shadows off the trees and gravestones, making dark sentinels out of the statues. More than once he imagined someone was waiting for him at a turn in the path, or he mistook the moonlight glinting off a marble headstone for the flicker of a flashlight.

At last he arrived at his uncle's grave. The wreaths and sprays of flowers formed a little mound over the spot where the coffin lay buried. Marc stood still, deeply moved.

Horace Guillon. Now there was a man who would have loved to join the people of Erymede. His philosophy had been so similar to theirs.

Marc went to the tombstone. The doctor's name hadn't yet been engraved on it. He knelt before it on the left side and explored the base of the stone with his fingers. The ground was hard, and Marc had difficulty digging below the surface. It seemed sinister work, scratching about in the soil where his aunt lay, but it had to be done. Marc knew he couldn't back out.

His hands were black with half-frozen earth, and he still hadn't found a thing. He was on the alert, but the only noise he heard was the nocturnal hum of the city and, every so often, the distant rumble of a truck passing on Cote-des-Neiges Road. To the east, the sky was rapidly becoming lighter.

Finally Marc's fingers struck something smooth. He dug around it, then pulled with all his strength. It was a transparent plastic envelope, smeared with black dirt. Inside was a manila envelope that contained the microfiche. Marc was so happy to have found it that he got up without filling in the small hole he had dug.

As he was moving away from the grave, he thought he heard a noise, like a car door being shut. But the sound was so muffled Marc wasn't sure he'd really heard it. He looked around, but saw nothing.

Nevertheless he quickened his pace along the hilly path towards the spot where he'd entered the cemetery. The silence had that special quality of early morning, a tranquillity peculiar to those first hours of the day. The cemetery was bathed in watery grey light; mist blurred the more distant trees.

All of a sudden Marc heard a voice. He turned and saw four men bending over the hole beside his uncle's grave. Marc recognised them all too well: Major Gagnon, Prevost and the two RCMP agents who had trailed him last evening.

Just as Marc noticed them, Gagnon spotted him, despite the distance and the gloom. Their eyes met. Then Marc turned on his heel and fled as he heard the major shout.

Marc didn't have to turn around to know that they were chasing him. They suspected that he had the microfiche on him. Now that they cared more about Doctor Guillon's notes than about Marc, he was entirely dispensable. They knew he'd never cooperate with them. They might even lock him up to make sure he never went to the press with the story.

Marc ran with all his might, clutching the plastic envelope in one hand. He heard the pounding of his pursuers behind him. There was no chance of escape. The younger men were in good shape; their stamina was better, and their stride surer. If he had been in better health he might have had a chance, but with his heart defect Marc simply couldn't sustain the effort. Even climbing the ski hill minutes earlier had brought him to the verge of fainting.

His heart felt like a caged animal desperate to escape. His chest hurt and he inhaled in ragged gulps. Already the edges of his vision were growing hazy and indistinct. In the half-light of early day he could barely make out the contours of the path. The trees and monuments on either side of him seemed to sway and wobble.

The men were quickly gaining on him. Then suddenly, Marc realised they weren't alone. Shadowy figures were running at him from the front. He had fallen into a trap!

He tried to veer off to the left, but even as he registered the idea, he felt his heart burst in his chest. He cried out as he lost his footing, then fell face first into the grimy snow and saw no more. As he lost the thread of consciousness, he felt the final throbbings of his ruptured heart.

Chapter Nine
Rescue

In the quiet moments of dawn, a drama was being played out in the silent cemetery. Like a wild creature hunted by a pack of hounds, a boy collapsed and died. His pursuers stopped in their tracks as they spotted four strangers running towards them. Two men and two women, all less than average height, and all dressed in ordinary fashion.

The police officers froze for a moment, taken completely by surprise. The four people all held strange-looking pistols in their hands. The cold air buzzed with barely audible sound, and pale rays of light struck the policemen. They swayed and fell to the ground like drunks.

Carl Andersen issued his orders: "Give them amnesia treatment and leave them here. Then report to the helicopter station. Phong, come with me."

As he spoke, he knelt over Marc's body. He turned Marc over and saw the boy's face creased with pain. He took hold of his wrist to check Marc's pulse and felt the last faint flutters of life. "Dead," he thought to himself, clenching his jaw.

He gathered Marc's lifeless form, as calm as a sleeping child, and started running in the direction from which he had come, followed by the woman named Phong. He knew that the two other members of the commando unit would complete their work calmly and efficiently. They'd inject the dozing police officers with drugs that would obliterate all recollection of the preceding ten or twelve hours.

Carl Andersen had left the shuttle conveniently hidden in the cemetery itself, on a flat strip of land where decaying flowers and wreaths were piled. Landing in the middle of an urban centre like Montreal was a risk Erymeans rarely took. In theory, the optical screens ensured the shuttle's invisibility, but certain luminous effects were inevitable. There was always a risk that they'd be spotted.

In the pearly grey shades of dawn, the shuttle was all but invisible. A faint shimmering in the air and an almost imperceptible phosphorescence betrayed the presence of an optic screen, but you had to look very carefully to detect it. A few meters away, you could pick out moving reflections, as if light were playing over rippling water. One or two meters away, the craft became visible, but its outline remained hazy and shifting, like a mirage.

Tram Phong reached the shuttle before Carl, who was carrying Marc's body. She opened the airlock and let down the gangway. Then she and Carl lifted the boy inside.

Carl sat the boy down and lowered the back of one of the seats to make a temporary bed. He told Phong, who had seated herself at the controls, "Destination Argus, direct flight, maximum velocity. Request communications link with medical personnel on Argus."

He could already feel the shuttle lifting off rather abruptly. Marc's head nodded limply. Carl's eyes were damp and his throat was tight with anger at the senseless murder, but he had no time to waste. He reached up and pulled a first-aid kit from a compartment in the cabin wall.

He passed a radioscope over Marc's chest. After some fine tuning, an image of his heart appeared on the little monitor. It was easy to spot the rupture of the left ventricle where it joined the aorta. Carl Andersen bit his lower lip at the sight: the organ had literally exploded under the strain.

But it wasn't too late to save the brain. The heart had stopped beating a mere two or three minutes ago. Soon, the brain cells, cut off from the crucial supply of blood, would begin to perish. When this happened, death was irreversible. Carl took a resuscitation apparatus out of the kit. It was designed to serve as a temporary heart and lung together, and featured a bundle of flexible plastic tubes fitted with hollow tips. Carl had never used the apparatus on a real person before. He took a deep breath and stuck the tubes into Marc's neck to hook up with the carotid arteries and jugular veins.

He turned on the machine. Gently, automatically adjusting pressure and rate, the circulator began to pump blood and oxygen through the body. This was only a temporary measure, enough to ward off brain death for a limited time only, but it was the best Carl could do under the circumstances.

Carl passed the encephalograph over the boy's head. The brain was functioning! It had slowed down, as if Marc were in a coma, but it was working. On the encephalograph's mini-screen, faint brain waves fluctuated, showing that electrical activity was still occurring. Carl Andersen breathed easier.

He went to the front of the cabin. Tram Phong pointed to a video screen from which the dark face of a middle-aged woman looked out.

"Doctor Sriva," she announced.

Sai Sriva was the director of medical services on Argus and the most skilled surgeon on the Moon. Carl described the state of the victim in as detailed a manner as possible, then calmly answered questions the doctor put to him. It didn't take long for Doctor Sriva to come up with a diagnosis.

"It's an extremely serious case," she said. "Especially with massive hemorrhaging in the thorax. The heart transplant will have to be performed on Erymede. We're simply not well enough equipped here. In the meantime, we must repair the damage done by the internal bleeding, replace the blood he's lost and, most importantly, connect the patient to an artificial heart to get his circulation going again. I'll requisition the astrobus that's just about to leave for Erymede. We can install an operating room with all the necessary equipment for intensive care. I'll personally direct the medical team."

Doctor Sriva issued a few more instructions for keeping Marc alive. Carl busied himself with the medical tasks while Tram Phong contacted the Argus astroport authorities to make sure the astrobus's departure would be delayed.

* * *

The boy's face and hands had been scrubbed clean. If you disregarded the tubes emerging from his neck, he could have been sleeping peacefully. This was an illusion, of course. Marc's heart no longer functioned and his lungs were useless and collapsed.

Sitting at the boy's side, Carl fiddled distractedly with the envelope of microfiches he'd found clutched in Marc's hand. Carl felt responsible for his death. He should have insisted on accompanying him to the cemetery. But it was too late now. At least he'd had the foresight to request a shuttle and a commando unit from the regional base in Maine. He'd had a hunch that it wouldn't be wise to underestimate the RCMP and the armed forces. Men like that didn't give up easily when they'd set their sights on a goal. The microfiches was obviously very important to them. Carl's hunch had proven correct.

But good hunches didn't solve everything. Marc was in critical condition, barely clinging to life. If he died, Carl would be deeply affected. He had initially approached Marc with the sole objective of recruiting him, but soon after they'd met, he began genuinely to like him. Maybe it was because Marc seemed lost and lonely, trapped in a family where his parents didn't seem to care for him, and where all his time was spent studying and working. Carl saw that Marc needed a friend or a big brother, as well as a chance to escape the intolerable conditions of his life. Erymede would have meant a new, enriching existence for Marc. But now, the future seemed quite uncertain for the boy whose heart was no longer beating.

* * *

The astrobus was preparing for take-off when the emergency call came through. Passengers were informed of the situation and willingly gave up their seats; they knew another astrobus would be arriving in six hours. They helped the medical team load equipment and convert the ship's cafeteria into an operating room. Everything was ready in less than an hour, and the astrobus, now transformed into an ambulance left the moon in earnest.

Twenty minutes later it connected with the shuttle in space. The computers on the two craft worked in tandem, accomplishing a hook-up so perfect there was no need for deceleration. The shuttle nosed its way into a specially designed bay on the astrobus, and hydraulic devices then clamped the shuttle firmly in place. Through the airlocks, Marc was carried into the astrobus on a self-propelled stretcher that coasted one meter above the decks of the craft. Once the transfer had been effected, Tram Phong, alone in the shuttle now, guided it back to the regional base in Maine.

While Marc was being brought into the makeshift operating room, the thrusters on the astrobus shot out bright plumes of plasma, driving the vehicle to speeds undreamt of on Earth.

For Carl, sitting alone in the main cabin of the astrobus, a long wait had begun.

Chapter Ten

Erymede

There were confused awakenings, then long periods during which Marc drifted in and out of consciousness, with muffled perceptions of his surroundings. The room in which he lay became vaguely familiar, a shadowy place where the subdued lighting had a warm amber tone. He did not think, he did not remember, feeling content with the slow passage of time.

At times, Marc was aware of people nearby, misty figures in pastel shades. There were faint murmurings, and sometimes a voice spoke to him, but he couldn't make out the faces and the words seemed meant for someone else. He had a vague feeling that these people meant him well and he did his best to smile.

* * *

When Marc opened his eyes and managed to focus his sight, he got the first clear view of the place where he lay. The ceiling was low, the room was small, the walls panelled with a strange material that looked like very dark wood streaked with purple. His bed was narrow, hard but comfortable, and had gold-coloured sheets.

There was no white, anywhere. Even the ceiling was a creamy almond colour. He wasn't in a hospital. And yet above the head of his bed, an array of instruments was trained on him, connected to a kind of panel. They looked like microphones hanging on flexible stems. A series of digital displays and undulating lines shone from the panel, which also contained a couple of darkened monitors.

For the first time in a long while, Marc could think clearly, and even attempt to use his memory. Little by little things came back to him. He remembered the events leading up to his loss of consciousness: the chase, falling, out of breath, with a painful sense of his heart tearing itself apart within him. But then ...

He was dressed in pyjamas, with the top taped shut in front by velcro bands. He opened it gingerly and looked at his chest. Two pink scars striped the skin: one long and vertical, just to the left of his breastbone, the other horizontal, shorter, crossing right over the first. The scars were closed. He couldn't even make out the stitches, but they left deep gullies in his flesh. Judging by the scar tissue, the operation had occurred days, probably weeks, ago.

So he had undergone heart surgery. Yet his cardiologist had told him only a month ago that his situation was hopeless. Had medical science made such progress in a single month?

Of course not. Surgery on Earth still lacked the technology to repair a heart like his. But on Erymede.... Could it be that he was on Erymede? He tried to lift himself up to see where he was. But he felt dizzy and the pain in his chest sprung up again.

The door in front of him slid open. A woman in a pale green smock entered.

"And now you understand," she said, "why you must rest in bed, young man."

She spoke in the straightforward friendly manner of a seasoned physician.

"Can't I even sit up?"

Marc realised an incredible thing. The doctor had addressed him in a foreign language and he'd understood every word she'd said. What was more, he had managed to answer her in the same clipped consonants she'd used. He was speaking Erymean!

"I'm on Erymede," he whispered, hardly daring to believe it.

"You've been here more than a month," the doctor informed him, propping him up in the bed.

"How did I learn Erymean? I've only just regained consciousness."

"Hypnopedagogy, my friend. While you slept, you listened to a pre-taped language course. Your subconscious mind did all the work."

Marc reflected on this astonishing piece

of information while the woman examined the medical panel and typed several questions on a wall-mounted keyboard. Answers soon flashed onto one of the monitors.

"Well, well," she said, smiling. "This says you're coming along very nicely."

"You operated on me a month ago?"

"Did I say that? No. We gave you a new heart six days ago. We had a lot of preparation to do beforehand. We don't often do this type of procedure and we were out of practice. On Erymede, congenital defects are very rare, and usually they're identified before birth."

"I've got a new heart?" exclaimed Marc.

"You wouldn't have gone too far with what was left of the old one."

"Tell me what happened."

"Do you know much about medicine?"

"Not really," Marc admitted.

"I'll keep it simple, then. On Earth, artificial organ transplants aren't yet possible, and there's a moratorium on some organ transplants because of the medical phenomenon of rejection.

"We've gotten around these problems by perfecting a biosynthetic substance for transplant surgery. We create it in the laboratory from human tissue. It has many properties of organic matter, but of course it isn't alive. In your specific case, we used tissue from your old heart to get the right genetic code. The heart we made won't be rejected by your body because your immune system will not perceive it as a foreign substance."

"But it is artificial?"

"Yes. Its pulse rate is controlled electronically by a device about the size of a grape. It's powered by a tiny battery which should last, in theory, at least, a hundred and thirty years. It took us almost thirty days to make the heart, to cultivate it, I should say, because we grew it right in the laboratory, like a plant. We soaked it in a liquid rich in nutrients, we radiated it, then stimulated it with electrical current. We moulded it and got it to the right consistency using temperature treatment and radiation emissions at specific wavelengths. In short, it's biochemical modelling work of the most delicate nature. Modeling flesh, as it were onto a frame."

Marc stared at his chest in disbelief. He felt a bit of disgust at the thought of the strange object embedded deep within him. This story of cultivating a substance both man-made and organic sounded like the experiments of some new Doctor Frankenstein. This monstrous organ in him wasn't quite alive, yet it wasn't entirely mechanical. It beat steadily like a living thing nestled among Marc's real organs.

Doctor Melos — this was her name — watched the boy's reactions closely, and noted that he had turned white. She was familiar with the psychological shock that usually followed such transplants. Marc's case was special, because he'd never heard about the technique before, and hadn't given his consent before the operation. These obstacles to adaptation were easily overcome. A few hypnosis sessions would help Marc to accept that his new heart was nothing loathsome.

"You say I was operated on recently. How come the incisions are already closed and healed?"

"We have processes that quicken the formation of scar tissue and the mending of bones. We had to cut your ribs, of course, but they'll soon be as good as new."

The door opened once more and a light-haired young man entered, dressed according to the local style: form-fitting pants and a long-sleeved shirt with a Nehru collar, all in a dazzling white.

"Carl!"

"So they finally decided to wake you up!" the young man laughed gently.

He embraced Marc, a gesture the Erymeans reserved for very close friends. The warm greeting, the first Marc had experienced in five weeks of unconsciousness, made him feel almost at home. He was no longer alone among foreigners in an alien world. He had a friend and guide to stand by him.

Marc asked, "What do you mean, 'they woke me up?' Was I drugged?"

"It's called electronarcosis, or induced

sleep," the doctor answered. "We don't believe it's necessary for a patient to be conscious while he is in critical condition, or beginning his convalescence. Asleep, he can avoid pain. Complete rest also speeds recovery. For instance, in the four weeks preceding your operation, we wanted to spare you the frightening sight of all those tubes sticking out of your chest, attaching you to the pump that served as a temporary heart."

Carl sat on the edge of the bed and put his hand on Marc's scarred chest. "Hmm," he said, "The new heart seems to be beating just beautifully."

"Marc should be very grateful to you," the doctor said. Then, turning to him, she began the story of his rescue. "You owe him your life," she said softly. "You were dead when he found you in that Montreal cemetery. Clinically dead. Your heart had literally burst."

Marc's eyes were round as saucers. He looked at Carl, then at the doctor. Doctor Melos described the measures Carl had taken to save his brain tissue and re-establish circulation with an artificial heart.

Marc was extremely moved. He'd been dead, yet he remembered nothing of the incident. He knew only how much he owed Carl. Carl had given him back his life. Because he had reacted so quickly and efficiently, Marc was here today. He took the young man's hand and squeezed it tightly.

"Okay, okay," the doctor said. "Let's not get over-dramatic. As of tomorrow, young fellow, you start an intensive exercise programme.. to get your muscles back in shape and your new heart into good working condition."

Marc gazed pensively at the pink scars running across his chest, trying in vain to discern some external sign of a heart beat. Nothing suggested that beneath his skin lay one of the greatest inventions of medical science. For Marc Alix, the new heart beating steadily within him was truly a symbol of the new life that lay ahead.

Read These Other Books in The Black Moss Young Readers' Library Series!

Also By Daniel Sernine...

Argus Steps In
Translated by Ray Chamberlain

Two youngsters vacationing in a Scottish medieaval castle shrouded in legends of dragons and curses. It belongs to the girl's grandfather, Trevor MacKinnon, a retired NATO general. The teenagers come to suspect that someone is held captive in the dungeon..

They are enlisted to help Marc and Carl (from Those Who Watch Over the Earth) in a secret mission which involves invisibility shields, dart guns and soporific gas grenades, as well as small shuttlecrafts acting as helicopters, to pluck the captive from the castle and his son from a frigate on the rough North Sea.

ISBN 0 88753 214 4 $5.95

Scorpion's Treasure
Translated by Frances Morgan

Luc and Benoit, teenage sons of farmers in the village of Neuborg near Quebec in 1647 New France, discover a mysterious cave. Then they witness the arrival by night of a mysterious ship and the unloading of heavy bags which the sailors take to the cave. A second visit to the cave confirms that it's a treasure.

How Luc and Benoit become involved with the captain who has left his treasure at Neuborg, and how their lives are endangered as a result make for an absorbing tale.

ISBN 0-88753-211-X $5.95

The Sword of Arhapal
Translated by Frances Morgan

In the small town of Neubourg near Quebec, the magical sword Arhapal is stolen.

Guillaume and Didier, two teenagers from Neuborg, begin investigating the theft. Didier gains access to the manor where the sword is hidden. His efforts to regain the sword, sometimes aided and sometimes threatened by unseen watchers, lead him into great danger. As he finds himself trapped in the cellars of the manor with a madman clutching the Sword Arhapal and rushing his way, it seems doubtful that he will survive.

ISBN 0 88753 212 8 $5.95

...And These Other Titles...

Beyond the Future
By Johanne Massé
ISBN 0 88753 210 1 $5.95

Lost Time
By Charles Montpetit
ISBN 0 88753 208-X $5.95

The Invisible Empire
By Denis Côté
ISBN 0 88753 213 6 $5.95

Shooting for the Stars
By Denis Côté
ISBN 0 88753 215-2 $5.95